GW00734415

ELEPHANTS CAN'T HIDE FOREVER

A MIKE TOBIN STORY

BY PETE PLENGE

Published by New Generation Publishing in 2012

Copyright © Peter Plenge 2012

First Edition

CHAPTER 1

THE BANK, 2003

St. Albans has always felt it should be the County Town of Hertfordshire. With its city title, majestic cathedral, Roman ruins and connections with Julius Caesar to name but a few reasons, it was and is far more worthy of premium status than the rather shabby town of Hertford, which had been bestowed with that honour shortly after the signing of the Magna Carta at Runnymede a thousand years previously. Well things had changed between the two towns over the millennium, for St Albans the road and rail infrastructure could not be better, access to Luton airport, M25, M1, A1M and the high speed rail link to St. Pancras and Farringdon were all there.

St. Albans was a place where people could get to where they needed to be quickly. Unlike most towns, from the centre of St. Albans you could be thirty miles away in as many minutes, and that brought affluence, wealth and Danny Gallagher to the city.

Danny Gallagher had done his research well. Each morning that St Albans held its market Danny and Madge, his wife of twenty five years, had left their home in Kent at 3.30am and driven up to St. Albans via the fruit and flower market at Nine Elms where they collected the forthcoming day's produce, and opened up their market stall for business by 7.30am. They kept themselves to themselves, never stopping for an early evening drink at the trader's local, but quietly packing up and driving back to Kent. In fact they were so innocuous that the other market stall holders wouldn't have recognised them should they have ever decided to call into the Red Lion.

Every Wednesday and Saturday was market day The main road through town St. Peter's Street was always full with market stalls, and this was a place that was good business for the wheelers and dealers of the market world, who plied their trade in their characteristically jovial fashion. The good people of St. Albans loved the market with its varied stalls and cockney banter from the traders.

In between the fresh soap stall and the quality watches for under a fiver, directly opposite Barclays Bank, was the fruit and vegetables stall that Danny Gallagher had been waiting to become vacant since he had selected St. Albans as his number 1 target. The stall had been operating for about 6 months and when the current occupier, that being Danny Gallagher, had been allocated the pitch, the Market Trading Manager had fleetingly thought it a bit strange that the lessee seemed more keen on the position of the stall than what chattels he intended to sell; however, this was soon forgotten when the fruit and veg appeared and the market needed another stall of this type. The quality of the goods was excellent and the rent was always paid with no fuss.

Mrs. Parkinson had discovered the stall in its first week of opening, liked the goods and liked the cheeriness of the owners; they were always polite and not as brash or as loud as the other people on the veg stall one hundred metres down towards the clock tower.

"Five bananas, a pound of grapes, six apples and one of those nice looking pineapples?" Mrs. Parkinson asked of Madge Gallagher on this particular September Wednesday morning at 11.23 am. "And where's your charming husband today?" she added

"Morning, love, he's just tidying up round the back" replied Madge Gallagher.

Danny Gallagher was indeed round the back, and he appeared to be tidying up; with his brush in hand no

4

one would have given Danny a second glance. Danny, however, was on high-octane. After six months of watching the bullion truck delivering to Barclays Bank at various times, things were falling into place. Danny was now convinced he had spotted a pattern, in what was designed to be random. If the bullion vehicle arrived today at 11 30am, he would not be serving Mrs Parkinson much longer.

At 11 30am, as Mrs Parkinson was admiring her fresh pineapple, a dark blue armoured security van pulled up directly opposite the fruit and veg stall. Two security guards climbed out, leaving one inside, and started carrying the cash into the bank that was to pay the various factory workers of St. Albans the next day. Danny felt the adrenalin hit his brain. This was conclusive proof that there was a pattern to the cash delivery at Barclays. He could now implement phase two of his plan.

Chapter 2

Danny Gallagher, August 1983

It was the late summer of 1983 and both Gallagher brothers were sitting in the bar of Sammy Gallagher's club down in Malaga.

"There's someone wants to meet you," Sammy said to his brother Danny, and when Sammy said 'someone wants to meet you', Danny knew it was a serious matter, and hopefully a big pay day.

Danny didn't like the Costa Del Crime; he was two years out of a long year stretch in HMP Wormwood Scrubs, and still wore the pallor of a man who had been incarcerated for a lengthy span. He thought the place was vulgar, and the bars were full of faces he had shared recreation with back on the wing in the Scrubs, home from home in more ways than one. What Danny did like about this place was his brother. Although they lived in different countries, they were still very close, and his brother's connections with the underworld were second to none. Sammy knew every villain in South London, indeed had worked with most of them, and now that he had moved out and bought this bar in Spain, he had a continuous flow of visitors from mainland Britain as well as the regulars who lived in their gated homes up in the hills, all of them villains. Sammy's bar had become a Mecca for the criminal fraternity who liked to flaunt their ill gotten wealth in the bars around town. Danny knew anyone seeing him in his brother's bar would know he was looking for work.

John Illes, also known as Mouse amongst his friends and the flying squad of New Scotland Yard, due to his pure physical presence, at 6ft 7ins and 260lbs of muscle, approached Danny from behind. Danny was hardly a small man himself, 3ins past 6ft, but Mouse dwarfed over him as he tapped him on the left shoulder and agilely nipped to his right like a kid's playtime joke.

"Fuck me, Mouse, you made me jump," said Danny, who had watched the Mouse approach in the bar mirror and turned to his right before the man had positioned himself.

"Same old Danny, smart as fuck, but plays the twat," said Mouse, "good to see you never lost it in the shovel."

"Thanks John" said Danny knowing how respectful it was to alternate between a man's nickname and his real name. "So what brings you down here, John? Have you bought a place so you can be near your mates?"

"Actually, Danny," said Mouse "I've no inkling to live in Spain; I love London, in any case Cathy wouldn't leave her mum, so that's it." Everyone knew Cathy Illes ruled the Mouse; unlike so many of his contemporaries John had stayed faithful to Cathy in the ten years they had been married, and she to him, and what's more everyone respected him for it.

Mouse continued: "It's you I've come to see Danny. I told Sam to give me a shout when you got here. So I jumped on a plane and got into Malaga two hours ago and here I am."

Danny's pulse quickened; he knew Mouse was looking for a reaction, and he needed to stay cool. Luckily the inadvertent warning his brother had given him earlier about someone wanting to see him had put him on guard. This was not an occasion for smart arsed remarks. So Danny looked Mouse straight in the eyes, and as was his way, got straight to the point.

"I guess we need to go somewhere very private then," he said.

"You guessed right, Danny boy" replied John. "Sammy has shut the VIP Suite tonight, so grab us a couple of beers and let's head up there."

The VIP suite of Sammy's bar, which Sammy had named The Crayfish after the watering hole back home, was discreet and opulent. Both men were as comfortable here as they were back in the other Crayfish, on the South London estate where they grew up, with its sawdust on the floor each Saturday night to soak up the blood that would inevitably be split by some unlucky soul before closing time. However, both knew the conversation that was coming was going to be for each other's ears only. So they sat closely in the middle of the empty room with an eye on the door although both guys knew that, if necessary, Sammy would stop the Four Horsemen of the Apocalypse from butting in.

John began, "Danny, it's true I've come to Spain especially to see you, and quite simply I am in the final stages of planning a job that's going to net us over 3 million. I've got a part for you and when it's gone down, and the old bill are crawling over every snout in town, I don't want anyone remembering seeing us together in the smoke, before the event."

Danny nodded sagely. This was typical of Mouse's good thinking and good planning. This was why John Illes was The Man and when The Man came calling, you were involved, simple as that.

"Go on," said Danny, his mouth getting dry in anticipation of what he was hoping to hear.

"Here's the deal then," replied Mouse, taking a long swig of beer. "You remember Brian Robinson I trust?" Mouse wasn't able to stop a lopsided grin forming.

A few years earlier, Danny had been the wheels man on a blag in Slough. Danny had driven up to the bank at exactly the time Brian Robinson was hastily departing,

8

having withdrawn £300k, not with his cheque book either but with an up and over sawn off shot gun. A member of the public decided to be a hero, and rugby tackled Brian. What Danny should have done then was floored the throttle and got out of there, leaving Brian rolling on the pavement and the other two in the bank. But he didn't, he got out and went to Brian's aid. Another member of the public also steamed in and all hell was let loose. Before they could shake off the do-gooders, the Sweeney turned up, collars were felt, and the boys all got a one way ticket to the Scrubs.

"I think I can picture him." Danny said sardonically. It was always taken as a given that the public never got involved; when there was violence afoot they just shit themselves and then boasted about it when they were safe, and for two Joes to wade in, there was more likelihood of the second coming but it had happened, and they had all got banged up for it.

However, if one good thing did come of it, it was that Danny had won the respect of all the lags doing their bird alongside him. When word got round the nick that Danny had sacrificed his freedom to help his mates, he was soon elevated to celebratory status on the wing and no one bothered him for the duration; even the Rastas gave him slack, and more importantly, the real big fish like Mouse considered him sound. It would be fair to say that Danny's act of loyalty eight years ago was why John Illes was now about to offer him a piece of the action. and unknown to both of them, a piece of history.

Mouse continued, "Well, Danny, Brian's got this brother-in-law name of Tony Black. He's a security guard at a bonded warehouse at the back of T4 at Heathrow, somehow he got talking to Brian about his shit financial state, and one thing led to another, and it turns out he's got access to all the security systems and even a key for the front door, he knows when there's any heavy duty money coming in and not only that, but he's willing to assist us in getting in and out."

"OK, that's fine," said Danny "But you know what these types are like, when the heat's on he's bound to get a tug from the old bill as he works there. And what's to say that after ten minutes of questions he won't crumble and sing like a bird to save his own skin, leaving us in the shit."

"Fair point Danny", replied Mouse. "I've already thought of that, and that's why I am here, and as far as the others are concerned no one makes contact with Brian, so the brother-in-law knows the only person he gets to see and talk to regarding this blag is Brian, so if he fucks up and opens his mouth it's his sister's brother he grasses and no one else. Not only that, but you know if Brian is collared he will keep quiet. Jesus, he owes us, and more particularly, he owes you."

"So what's my part?" Danny asked.

"Well" said Mouse, lowering his tone. "There are six of us going into the warehouse and vault, the cash we now know is coming will be delivered in at five am on the 26th November and we go in ten minutes after the shift changes at 6 40am. I anticipate loading the money, securing the guards, and getting out in fifteen minutes. You, Danny, will be the back up wheels and first change of motors, so I want you in position five minutes away down on Stanwell Moor. We'll come to you, bung the cash in your motor, you high tail it down to my lock up in Bexley. I'll give you the address on the day; you leave the van inside the lock up and make yourself scarce, ideally get yourself booked on the 11am flight back here. We will divvy up a week before Christmas, how does that sound?"

"Sounds good to me," said Danny, a bit disappointed that he wasn't on the front line operation, still, he was in, and knew unless he fucked up big time, he was in for life. Danny continued, "So who are the other guys, apart from you and Brian?" he asked.

Mouse took a long breath before replying. "Well firstly there's Eric Logan, he's going to be the muscle backing me up."

Fucking hell, thought Danny, he's a right psycho. Eric Logan, also known as Bones had always had and enjoyed a reputation as a nutter. A couple of years younger than Danny, they had been at the same school, and, even then, Danny had been canny enough to give him a wide berth. Bones Logan was the silent type who didn't pick a fight; he just started it, no signs, and no warnings, just for the hell of it. What elevated Mr. Logan into John's team was the fact that Bones Logan had dealt with a very bad problem a couple of years back, in a very discreet way, and only a handful of people ever knew, and of course Mouse was one of them.

The story was that Eric's sixteen year old daughter Loretta, or Loll to her friends and family, had been out in the Cray on a Saturday night, doing what sixteen year olds do, when two toe rags from Catford, having nicked a set of wheels, had decided to come over to Sidcup for a bit of action in their newly acquired AMG Merc 600s. Unfortunately for Loll and her mate Ruby, and as it happened, unfortunately for them. The two car thieves spotted the girls disappearing off the high street and heading down a quiet alley to take a pee. Both lads had jumped out of the Merc and followed them. Ruby was already squatting down, and the first of the lads commented, "Glad to see you've got your knickers off, that'll save me a job."

Both girls were startled, but Loll was quick to reply: "Fuck off arseholes."

One of the toe rags pushed Ruby over as the other

11

approached Loll. Loll, daughter of Bones Logan, was no shrinking violet; neither was she in any doubt what these lads were after, and she had to act fast. As the boy approached her, she pulled a nail file from her bag and lashed out at him, opening a deep gash from the corner of his eye to just under his nose. She then gave him further verbal abuse. Both toe rags launched into the girls with a feral ferocity, and very shortly had overcome their initial resistance and beaten them senseless; it wasn't exactly what they had in mind when they followed the women down the alley, but they were satisfied with their work, and duly left the scene looking for more sport.

It was 3am in a local gambling den when Bones took the call from his wife Debby.

"Eric, Loll's in the intensive care unit Sidcup general, she's been attacked, get here fast," he was instructed.

Bones, who doted on his daughter, threw what was the winning hand of the poker game over the pot at the speiler he frequented on most Saturdays, and drove like a bat out of hell to his daughter's bedside. Half an hour after Eric's arrival, the duty locum addressed Eric and Debby as he finished examining Loll, "She's going to be fine, her spleen is bruised and there are two broken ribs. The cuts on the face won't leave a scar at her age, so we'll move her out onto the general ward and she can go home in a couple of days," he said.

Eric just managed a nod but his thunderous expression never changed. Debby, who had grown up in a very hard environment and had seen plenty of broken bones in her time, was not about to break down either.

"Thank you, doctor, and please thank all your staff" she said, as she offered her outstretched hand, leaving the locum under the impression that he should now go and leave the husband and wife alone, which he duly obliged.

With the room to themselves, Debby spoke to Eric:

"Loll's going to be fine, leave her with me, go and do what you have to, come home when its over."

Eric Logan walked over to his daughter's bedside, ran the palm of his hand through her matted and bloodied hair, and left. There was only one thing on his mind - retribution.

Three weeks later, Colin Winn was sitting across the desk from a pretty assistant in the local Thomas Cook travel agent on Bexley High Street. Colin was booking a surprise holiday for his wife and four children and he was very pleased with himself; this was not only going to be a holiday totally out of the blue for the family, but wait till he told them it was for two weeks in Lazaretto and all inclusive. Ok, when Bones Logan, his old school mate, had told him in no uncertain terms what he needed from him, he had initially shit himself, but fuck it, half an hour's work and he was sitting here with five large ones booking the holiday of a lifetime. *Wait till I pay for this in readies*, he was thinking, *that will get me respect.*

Colin was a truck driver; to be specific, a ready- mix concrete truck driver, and the past four months had been like thirty others, shuttling concrete from the batching plant in Swanley to the site of the new bridge spanning the Thames, a boring monotonous job that paid well but lacked variation. That was until yesterday, and yesterday there was variation. His last run of the day took him from the batching plant via a seedy back street garage in Erith where he had been instructed to report by his recent benefactor. As the whoosh of the air brakes signalled the truck was securely parked, Bones Logan appeared from the side door with two people Colin didn't know, and looking at

13

them, didn't want to either.

"Col, were going to be adding some cargo to the concrete, we know your load won't be tested because Dave here's had a little word with the checker on pillar thirteen where you're tipping, so all you got to do is make sure you get the load down the shaft, and not miss it, there's going to be two more loads straight behind you and everyone will want to go home, now give us a hand".

After the mutilated, charred remains of the two car thieves from Catford had been fed into the revolving drum of Colin Winn's cement mixer, the big guy with a false eye handed Colin his five grand with the menacing words, "You're a lucky man, five grand to spend on those four kids, keep them safe."

Colin had started his engine, but before he got out of sight pulled over and spewed his stomach out over his passenger seat. He had toughed it out at the garage, but had never seen a dead body before, let alone the remains of two people who had suffered so horrifically. Eric had said to the man with one eye, "He will keep stum, no fear." Half an hour later, the two bodies were tipped out of the mixer to fertilise the ground under the new bridge, undoubtedly not the first and not the last.

Of course, news of the highly secret operation spread like wildfire in the pubs and clubs of South London. Eric Logan had accredited himself well, and so Eric Bones Logan found himself invited onto the team, and batting with the big boys.

"Who else?" asked Danny.

"Well," replied Mouse "We've got Herbie Sparks on the alarms and cameras."

Danny knew Herbie, who had a legitimate electrical shop over the water in the borough of Chingford. He fitted security systems all over Essex, and there was no shortage of business on that manor, both to the great and good and to the not so good; the villains and the hoi-polloi all cherished their security, and Herbie had no qualms who he did business with. Furthermore, over the years had become a trusted part of several major gangs when a specialist like himself was required. "Good man," commented Danny.

"Yeah, invaluable" said Mouse, "And the last two are Martin Flint and John Bater." Both these men were known as Petermen in the trade, another specialist requirement in the art of bank robbery and the like, once again a trade that, like Herbie's, was running short of skilled personnel. As far as the general public were aware the Peterman was a safe cracker and John Illes needed two safe crackers on this job and these two were the best.

Both men had served and learnt their trade in the Royal Army Ordinance Corps. On leaving the Army they were now experts in all major aspects of munitions, including bomb disposal. They had taken their skills to the highest bidders, starting with legitimate employment in the major oil companies, who always required such men to clear areas of the world such as demilitarised zones, in order to safely deploy their field experts in the constant search for new oil deposits. As the two mercenaries gradually moved round the world, they soon discovered their unique knowledge commanded huge rewards for the not so legitimate enterprises that were involved in the business of bombs and really anything that exploded, and that included the criminal fraternity of their home country, the United Kingdom. Both men had built a common trust with the villains of England and Scotland, and were usually the first to be contacted when the need arose; certainly when Mouse was putting his team together they were the only two names he wanted.

"Well I don't know these last two, Mouse" said

15

Danny," but I guess you wouldn't employ monkeys."
Mouse grinned, enough said then.

"Do you mind if I ask what my share is?" Danny
enquired.

"Fair question" said Mouse. "It's the six of us that
are going in to the warehouse who are taking the most
risk, so I reckon that you're on for five percent, which
if it's three million, that's a hundred and fifty large
ones. How does that sound?"

"More than fair," agreed Danny, John Illes stuck his
huge hand out to Danny,

"Sorted then. Let's go downstairs and celebrate," he
grinned. At precisely 6.40am on the morning of
November 26th 1983, six armed and highly dangerous
men led by John Illes, The Mouse, walked through the
front doors of the Brinks Mat warehouse, Heathrow,
unaware they were about to become complicit in the
crime of the century

Chapter 3

War in Afghanistan

President George W Bush sat transfixed, staring at the bank of television monitors in front of him; it was the morning of September 11th 2001. He was aboard Air Force One, the presidential plane that he usually used to visit foreign countries. This morning, however, he had been performing administrative tasks in the oval office which was his sanctum within the White House, when the bright green hot phone shrilled into action. This was the line known only to six men, all heads of the various security services that jointly ensure the USA remains safe from hostile forces. This was the first occasion the phone had rung since J F Kennedy had answered it to be told the Russians were heading to Cuba with a batch of nuclear warheads back in the 1960s. The caller was John Robertson, head of National Security. John spoke calmly.

"Sir, I need you to listen carefully and do as I say. As I speak America is under attack from hostile but unknown forces- at 830am we took a scrambled call from a US Marshall aboard American Airlines flight 11 out of Boston. As you know sir, all US flights have unidentifiable Marshalls, well the Marshall's call was chilling, he said the plane he was travelling on had been hijacked by a group of men who seemed very well organised and had taken over the flight deck. He deduced at least one of the hijackers was a pilot. As National Security were deciphering the Marshall's call, a further call came in from United Airlines flight 175, also out of Boston. The US Marshall on this flight reported almost identical circumstances."

The President listened, a knot forming in his

stomach. "Mr President, I cannot emphasise how grave the situation is" said John Robertson. "We locked onto the two aircraft as soon as we heard the news; both had changed direction and were heading for New York City."

"My God," thought the president, not fully taking in what he was hearing.

The head of National Security took a deep breath.

"Sir, to bring you up to date, at 845 this morning, the United Airlines flight 11 crashed into the north tower of the World Trade Centre, at 905 the second plane crashed into the south tower. There are two other flights over America that we believe may also have been hijacked, destination unknown. Four F16s have been scrambled from Dulles and will, under instruction, shoot any aircraft out of the skies should we feel they are under hostile control." The time was now 9:30 am. "Mr President, America is under attack, we will keep you up to speed as events unfold, but firstly you must issue the Presidential order that we immediately go to DEFCON 1."

He paused a second to allow the ramification of these words to sink in. The USA, like most countries, has a prioritised list of alert statuses for its armed forces and other agencies, DEFCON 5 being no threat perceived and peace, escalating to DEFCON 1 which is imminent attack, requiring full mobilisation of all armed forces and major evacuation of cities under threat. The American authorities had not been in a DEFCON 1 situation since the Cuban missile crisis of 1963.

John continued, "Further, Mr President, you are to be escorted immediately to Air Force One, with other key staff including FLOTUS(the acronym for the president's wife: First Lady of the United States). Once Air Force One is airborne we will assess a safe destination, but at this moment in time that may have to be a friendly country."

As the conversation continued, the doors to the Oval Office burst open, and two fully armed Marines approached the President. War had been declared on the USA and the President had to be made safe; and so as respectfully as possible, the Marines escorted him with the utmost urgency to the waiting helicopter, which would whisk him to the safety of the Presidential 727 Jumbo. The United States was under attack, violators currently unknown.

President Bush sat motionless, engulfed in the horror of watching US citizens leaping from the burning buildings of the World Trade Centre. Since Air Force One had lifted off, the situation had become more extreme; the pictures on the screen of the burning towers of the World Trade Centre were the stuff of nightmares, but they had now been replaced by a CNN crew who were filming live pictures from Washington. American Airlines flight 77 had crashed into the Pentagon, the President watched in abject horror as a huge plume of smoke rose from the burning building. By now the world was watching the macabre events unfolding in the greatest country in the world, the United States of America. Both the Pentagon and the White House were being evacuated with extreme haste; the terrorists had the great Satan running scared.

10:05 am saw the south tower of the World Trade Centre collapse; like a deck of cards the massive symbol of American Capitalism slithered to the ground causing a huge cloud of rubble and dust to spread across the nearby streets.

The National Security and US agents that surrounded POTUS, The President of The United States, were frantically gathering information from the rows of electronic wizardry that filled every nook and cranny of Air Force One. Every satellite and listening device on the earth could be fed through the aircraft; each and every member of the team knew that when the atrocities of the day released their hold on POTUS, he would want answers and expect them.

Approximately ninety minutes into the flight of Air Force One, at 10.28am eastern seaboard time, the second tower of the World Trade Centre, which once stood tall and proud as a symbol of American prestige, came juddering ground ward. The President had watched enough. He had witnessed the unimaginable; America reduced to rubble by forces unknown. How, with all the resources America spent on its security, could this have happened, without so much as a whisper? He had just witnessed the mass murder of what must be thousands of Americans. POTUS rose from his chair and looked towards the hubbub of the personnel busy seeking and analysing the constant chatter of the surrounding machines spewing out the incoming intelligence from the world's security services. The President stood and gazed around the room and for two minutes he said nothing, and every man and woman stopped their work and an unnatural quiet descended.

Eventually the President spoke.

"Who did this John?" he asked in a barely audible voice. The head of national security looked the President in the eye and said:

"Sir our initial Intel has established that the organisation responsible for this is: Al-Qaeda."

"Go on" said POTUS.

"Al-Qaeda, Sir" said John Robertson to the President. The President's assembled people sat or stood in total silence. He continued: " Al-Qaeda is an Islamist group founded sometime between 1988 and 1989.We have known of their existence since its

20

inception when several senior leaders from the Islamic Jihad organisation joined forces with a wealthy Saudi extremist. Since then they've gone off the radar. Although several suicide bombings have been attributed to these people nothing has ever been proven and, unusually, nothing claimed."

The President pondered for a moment, you could hear a pin drop and John Robertson knew the President's next question, which he duly delivered.

"Who, John, is the leader of this organisation?"

"Osama Bin Laden Sir, is the Saudi benefactor," came the reply.

"And where might we find him?" demanded the President, at last re-capturing some of his fighting spirit.

"Afghanistan, Sir" came the reply.

The World entered a new phase.

Sixteen days later on the 7th October 2001, American forces invaded Afghanistan under the brief Operation Enduring Freedom. The aim was to bring Bin Laden and other high ranking members of Al-Qaeda to trial, destroy the entire organization and remove the existing rulers of Afghanistan, the Taliban.

Thirty two days later Major Mike Tobin, known as Nine Fingers to his comrades in the British SAS, was readying himself to answer the President's request.

Chapter 4

Nangarhar province, eastern Afghanistan

Gandamak is a village in eastern Afghanistan situated between the country's capital and the Pakistani town of Peshawa; a cold inhospitable settlement. Its only claim to fame, if you could call it fame, was that a hundred and fifty nine years previously, the First Afghan war was concluded there. On the afternoon of January 13th 1842, the British troops, who were retreating to India through the mountain passes having been overwhelmed in Kabul, made their last stand against the Afghan hordes in Gandamak. They were cut to ribbons; what with the cruel Afghan winter and cowardly British Officers they never stood a chance, and that was about the sum total of Gandamak's claim to fame.

Gandamak lies relatively close to the Tora Bora mountainous region of Afghanistan. The Tora Bora, or White Mountains, lie in the District of Nangarhar, only 50 kilometres west of the Khyber Pass, which joins Afghanistan to Pakistan.

The English and American press in the furore of post September 11th had all claimed that the mountains of Tora Bora contained a hotel -like bunker, where Osama Bin Laden and up to two thousand followers were holed up. The idea that the perpetrators of the horrific attacks on America were hiding in caves in the middle of Asia embedded itself into the American public. They wanted retribution, and George W Bush was not silly enough to deny them their bloodlust, indeed it was he who led the rallying cry for the heads of those responsible for the recent attacks. So it transpired, whether through fact or fiction no one will

22

ever know, that a report from the Secretary of Defence USA was leaked to the American press, stating that immediately post September 11th (or 9/11 as it was now referred to), Bin Laden had been picked up by a British AWAC(Airborne Early Warning and Control) spy plane, leaving Kabul, on a donkey no less, and heading for the impenetrable fortress of the Tora Bora mountains.

Like a recalcitrant child who can't get his own way and lashes out at the nearest thing, POTUS decided, probably carried along by the American groundswell that Bin Laden must perish in his mountain hideaway. He ordered a great force of bombers to systematically reduce the Tora Bora mountain range to dust, and those hiding underneath as well; even if Bin Laden wasn't there the World would see the full might of American anger when aroused and the good folks of the USA might start to feel good about themselves again.

Mike Tobin, British SAS Captain and his three comrades sat outside the café, in Sher Poor Square Gandamak.

They listened to the constant thunder of the B 52s dropping their deadly ordinance payload as they reshaped the landscape of the Tora Bora Mountains. Their mission was to destroy the members of Al-Qaeda hiding beneath.

It struck the four SAS troopers with great irony that this entire division of America's finest airborne was in fact wasting their time, as the quarry they so desperately sought to blast into eternity was, in fact, holed up in a house fifty metres from where they sat.

For fifteen days they had been sitting outside the café and at first they had attracted some minor attention. Dressed as Afghan farmers, and fully covered up for protection against the cold winter, they soon blended in with the indigenous population. Many

23

Afghan farmers now resorted to spending the majority of their days doing likewise, ever since the great Satan, the USA, had systematically destroyed their crops and income from the poppy fields.

The four members of the SAS snatch squad had walked into Gandamak from the Pakistan town of Peshawar, crossing the border at nightfall; little attention was paid to them in this remote and hostile environment. There was a constant stream of human flotsam crossing into and out of Pakistan. Whilst sitting outside the café, whiling away the time, they had kept a constant eye on the alleyway running off at right angles to the road they sat by. Nothing unusual had been observed; in fact to these highly trained individuals the very fact that nothing moved up or down this alleyway was in itself an indication that there was something unusual occurring, and that unusual occurrence was the fact that, providing GCHQ had not fucked up, Osama Bin Laden was sitting in the back room of the fourth house down the alley, safe in the knowledge that the distant rumble of the American bombers indicated no one had a clue where he really was.

It was the most extraordinary piece of luck that brought these four men into the lawless region of Eastern Afghanistan, and now as they waited for darkness to envelop the small village, they readied themselves for the snatch they had been planning which was to occur that evening.

Chapter 5

GCHQ (General Command Headquarters Cheltenham), 4 weeks previously

GCHQ sits just outside the town of Cheltenham. Local residents are aware of its existence but pay little attention to the comings and goings. Its function is to listen and monitor the constant chatter of the world at large. It can eavesdrop on every telephone conversation no matter what the contents or classification. GCHQ can filter the millions of phones calls which are made each second of every day through their massive computers, and discard the normal, but recognise those that may be less ordinary and deal with them accordingly; so if certain known numbers or words are used, this triggers an automatic segregation whereby these numbers are flashed to one of the waiting monitors manned by the team of trained listeners, who will then track the call and wait for further developments. The task is both tiresome and tedious for the watchers, as ninety nine percent of suspect calls turn out to be fruitless. It has always irked the British Security Service that GCHQ has been looked upon by the cousins across the pond at Langley as a somewhat provincial outfit which rarely contributes to world security, and they longed for an opportunity to prove they were actually the world's premier spymasters.

On this particular day in mid December 2001, all was about to change. Sally Dixon, recently recruited from Cambridge after obtaining a First in middle eastern languages, was sitting watching her screen display various low level chit chat emanating from the area covering the Gulf and north Tajikistan, when her screen went dead, immediately followed by a flashing red warning message which read 'incoming encrypted message, maximum status, area North East Afghanistan, delivery via Predator'

Sally had heard of these messages in the canteen when the staff met and swopped stories, but the truth was the last red flash had occurred 10 years or so earlier when a satellite had spotted 300 tanks with Iraqi markings going hell for leather towards the Kuwait border. Sally's training kicked in, she hit the panic button next to the monitor which would alert her departmental head sitting one storey above, and then logged into her two immediate neighbours' computers, both middle east experts, in case her screen crashed.

The vehicle that was about to deliver its life changing message to young Sally, was, to give it its full name, the Unmanned Aerial Vehicle Predator MQ-1, better known as a drone. Used by the British and American armed forces and security networks, it was a pilotless aircraft that could fly at altitudes of fifty thousand feet, watching and listening to what was occurring beneath it. It could observe enemy movements and in real time convey information to the front line soldier; furthermore it was capable of picking up radio and satellite messages no matter how smart the enemy on the ground thought he was being in evading their monitoring systems.

On this particular December morning, the Predator had been deployed in the region of Afghanistan known locally as the Safed Koh, or white mountains, otherwise known as the Tora Bora area; indeed most of the western world's military resources were focused on this region, for it was here that the American intelligence community were certain Osama Bin Laden had taken refuge following his departure from Kabul a couple of weeks earlier. The Predator, flying at thirty thousand feet, had just covered its third sweep of the day and was preparing to circle back when an unusually strong side wind blew it slightly off course. As it automatically readjusted its position, its flight took it over the village of Gandamak, and at that precise moment an encoded, encrypted message, reduced to a nano second by the sender on the ground, hit the sensors of the Predator with a ping no louder than a submarine using sonar would locate another vessel. The Predator's equipment locked into the location of the sender within five feet, and together with the electronic message, forwarded it to GCHQ's bank of satellite dishes and then on to the desk of Sally Dixon.

As the message hit Sally's console, a red faced John Watson, Sally's head of department had arrived having flown down the stairs at breakneck speed. He was immediately followed by the director of the facility, Margaret Fortune The rest of the floor had become very quiet, every person working that day within proximity of Sally sensed something very, very special had come in.

"Sally," said Margaret quietly, "Lock your machine down, then come up to the bunker," and then to the hushed room,: "That's all the excitement for today, ladies and gentlemen, but just let me remind you all, when you leave here tonight you are all bound by the official secrets act".

Margaret led the way to the secure operations room, known as the bunker for it was insulated by four feet of concrete side to side and top to bottom; if a nuclear strike hit GCHQ the bunker would survive, this however was not the reason it was so fortified. It had been designed for ultra top secret meetings, in the knowledge that no listening device could penetrate the walls. Sally had only heard of this sanctum, and now she found herself sitting in the rather eerie half light of

27

the bunker with two of the most powerful civil servants in the country.

Margaret booted up the computer that the message had been transferred to. As chief officer, she was more a politician than specialist, and so she gestured to John Watson.

"Open it up John, let's get it deciphered and see what we're dealing with," she said as if it was a can of baked beans she was asking to be opened. John Watson had been deciphering coded messages for twenty years and he was confident once he had opened this transmission he would have it cracked in no time.

After three hours of intense keyboard activity, John's monitor sprang to life, displaying the information they had been waiting for. Simultaneously the huge screen in the corner showed Margaret and Sally what John had unravelled. Covering the screen was what looked like a series of Arabic letters randomly scattered across the page.

"Can you read it?" Margaret asked Sally.

"Well," said Sally, "I can read the letters, but in the Arabic alphabet letters can be used as numbers and as far as I can make out this text is a mixture of letters and numbers."

"Right" said Margaret, "first things first, how long to get this into English so we can start working it out?"

Sally had no idea but what she did know was that Margaret would not accept such a negative answer.

"Two hours" said Sally.

"One maximum" was Margaret's reply.

Fifty eight minutes later, the three colleagues were looking at Sally's handiwork. From the ebullient moment of the message's arrival at GCHQ, to Sally's translation now on the screen before them, their mood had changed. They were looking, mesmerised, at a set of binary numbers interspersed with the odd random letter. This was a top secret covert message from a little house in the lawless district of Afghanistan and didn't make sense. John and Margaret, both seasoned professionals, sensed this may have a huge relevance in the war in Afghanistan; it was too coincidental that the message had been intercepted by the drone only 50 klicks from the Tora Bora mountains. This may take them days to decipher, by which time the sender of the message from Gandamak may have flown. John looked at Margaret, and for what seemed an eternity said nothing, thinking who in the world would be the best person to decipher this message, eventually one word left his mouth: "Rusty" he whispered, and Margaret nodded.

Chapter 6

Bletchley Park, an annex of GCHQ, 3am the next day

Professor Duncan Campbell, actually known as Rusty, was sleeping the sleep of babies. Like all geniuses sleep came easily, and when it came it was deep and dreamless, and so it must have been the tenth shrill of the phone that he finally released hold of his somnolent state and gruffly answered.

"This had better be good" he growled.

The reply came back: "Rusty, it's Margaret Fortune, we have a situation, category one, we need you in your office in ninety minutes, I'm boarding a helo in five minutes for Bletchley."

No more could be said on an unsecured line but Rusty Campbell instantly knew if the head of GCHQ was boarding a helicopter at 3am to fly to Bletchley Park the shit had truly hit the fan.

"I'll have the coffee on, Margaret" was his reply.

Bletchley Park is in fact a country estate, now surrounded by the city of Milton Keynes. It gained fame during the Second World War when it became the United Kingdom's main decryption establishment; the high level intelligence produced there was considered crucial to the war effort, and indeed the facility had been credited with shortening the war in Europe. Its most famous achievement was to decrypt and break the German Enigma cipher machine, although those in the know would argue that more importantly, the breaking of the German FISH High Command teleprinter ciphers, enabling the allied forces navy to plot and destroy the German U-boats ,was the single main factor in the allied victory.

What was not public knowledge was the fact that the unit was still very much active; albeit certain parts of the building were now open to the public, there were areas strictly off limits where the boffins still operated. Although the staff were massively reduced, the building contained the greatest mathematicians and polyglots the United Kingdom had ever reared.

Of these great academics, Professor Duncan Campbell was the best of the best; with his broad Scottish accent, and his unkempt flaming red hair and beard, he looked more likely to be found on the fields of Bannockburn than at this top secret institution. Looks can be deceiving, and no more so than in the case of Rusty Campbell. Twenty years previously he had flown through Cambridge achieving passes never before realised; his PHD on the 'Relativity of Numbers During The Formation Of The Universe' was considered a masterpiece, and changed the way astrophysicists looked at time and space. Duncan became Professor of Pure Mathematics at the age of twenty nine, the youngest ever, and was expected to remain in the hallowed halls of Cambridge as a lector of mathematics for the rest of his career. He even had his eye on the 100k prize money to be awarded to the first mathematician who could identify the latest binary number.

MI5, however, had other ideas; they had watched his development from an early age, and shortly after his PHD was published made their move. After several top level meetings with the hierarchy of the secret service, Professor Duncan "Rusty" Campbell joined the team of Crypto analysers at Bletchley Park, and settled into the world of secrecy and intrigue, far away from the university life he had thought was his destiny.

And so here he sat on this cold December morning, at the ungodly hour of 4.30am, waiting for Margaret

Fortune to arrive with what might be his greatest challenge. He couldn't wait.

Just as the coffee percolator hit boiling point, Duncan heard the whack whack of the helicopter's rotors, and walked out onto the frosted lawns of Bletchley Park. Margaret, rather ungainly as is the way of unseasoned passengers, alighted the chopper and made her way to over to Rusty.

"Duncan, good to see you again," she said through chattering lips.

"Likewise," came the reply. "Let's get you inside and warmed up."

Once inside Duncan's office, Margaret got straight to the point.

"Duncan, we have intercepted an encrypted message from Afghanistan. It may of course be nothing, but the region it came out of is too coincidental, and more importantly my instincts tell me it's something big."

Duncan knew the pleasantries were over. "Right," he said, "let's take a look."

Duncan had never failed to decipher a manuscript in his entire career, and as he gazed at the random letters and numbers before him his mind was working faster than the speed of light. At exactly 8.45am, four hours after Duncan had opened the message, he had cracked it and the two people sat staring at the decrypted message, in deep thought at what it revealed. Eventually Margaret opened her briefcase, pulled out a tiny piece of paper, flipped open her cell phone and punched in the numbers on the paper in front of her. After two rings the phone was answered.

"Tony Blair" came the reply

"Prime Minister," said Margaret in as even a voice as she could muster. "This is Margaret Fortune speaking. We have today intercepted a message from inside Afghanistan. If it is to be believed then we have the precise location of Osama Bin Laden."

Chapter 7

The war room, 10 Downing Street, two hours later

Prime Minister Blair sat alone in the war room of his official home, 10 Downing Street. Like Duncan Campbell, his minds was racing; if what he had been told was true, or even the fact that his senior civil servant from GCHQ had alerted him to the possibility, that the most wanted man on earth had been found, he knew what he had to do. He should have informed his counterpart in Washington, George Bush, but the Prime Minister was a politician and, having achieved the ultimate goal of First Office of the United Kingdom, a very clever politician. He knew the British public, and worse still the British press, had lost confidence in his administration, and him personally, following the debacle of the Iraq invasion in the pursuit of non existent weapons of mass destruction. The next general election was already all but lost, and if he was brutally honest with himself, he should fall on his sword sooner rather than later, and yet out of the blue suddenly an early morning phone call had given him a lifeline, a very risky lifeline but nonetheless an opportunity to save himself and his Government. So Mr. Blair had not called POTUS, neither had he called any members of the Strategic War Council; instead he arranged a very fast unmarked police car to bring Margaret Fortune from Bletchley to his office, and then made one call to the Army Barracks in Hereford known as Stirling Lines, home of 22 Regiment Special Air Service, Britain's top special forces cadre.

Major Sebastian Morley had been sitting at his desk when the call came in from the Prime Minister.

"Sebastian, something's broken," said Tony Blair "How fast can you get to London?"

Major Morley knew this meant half an hour ago. "One hour, sir" he replied, mentally computing where the nearest chopper was.

"Fine, straight to Downing Street please" came the reply.

Major Morley strode purposefully out of his office and could not conceal the wide grin he was sporting.

"Morning boss, what's put that smile on your face?" asked his adjutant.

"PM's summoned me," said the Major and that put a smile on the face of his junior NCO. There's nothing an SAS soldier likes more than trouble, and this, both men knew, was going to be big trouble.

Margaret was the first to arrive at 10 Downing Street, and after the usual pleasantries which lasted considerably longer than those earlier in the day with Duncan, she got down to business. For thirty minutes the PM said nothing, just listened as she talked and walked the PM through the day's developments. He finally spoke,

"Thank you Margaret, you have covered the situation extremely thoroughly. I believe, the message you have intercepted is bonafide and that we have located our man."

During Margaret's delivery of the known facts, the Major had arrived from Hereford, been shown in, and had listened to her telling the PM how she had encrypted a message which implied Osama Bin Laden was hidden up in a small Afghan village, and not the Tora Bora Mountains. He was sitting in the corner, half knowing and half hoping what would be coming next.

"Well Major, anything you need to know and your comments please" the PM inquired.

"No sir, I fully understand the situation," came the

reply. With that, the PM rose from his chair and paced the room for several moments, lost in thought but rapidly coming to a decision. He turned and faced Margaret.

"Margaret, "he asked, the tenseness now etched on his face, "How many people are aware of this document?"

"Excluding the three of us sir, there are three others two at GCHQ and one at Bletchley," replied Margaret.

"Can we guarantee their integrity in this matter?" asked the PM.

"Absolutely, PM, you have my personal commitment on the matter." Margaret's sincere if somewhat ominous reply convinced the PM of his course of action.

"In that case" he said looking directly at Major Sebastian Morley "Can your people get him out?"

"Yes, sir" was the answer.

"You have a one month window to extract the target, but be warned, Major, this has to be a Black Operation," the PM stated. Major Morley was not in the least put off by the PM's last comment. Any untoward publicity if there was a foul up, or the press got wind of things, the PM and the British Government would deny all knowledge of the mission and also have the Major's balls as well as his pension.

"That concludes our meeting then" the PM stated," Not of course that we've had a meeting" he remarked with that twinkle in his eye he usually saved for the media.

As the Major was being discreetly shown the back door exit, he reached inside his combat jacket, pulled out his cell phone and rang a number of a council house on a rather unsavoury estate in Gateshead.

"Hello," Mike Tobin answered in a slightly slurred voice

"Nine, I need you back in Hereford six am tomorrow," the Major ordered. "Sober" was his last word as he shut the phone down; just like Mike Tobin there was going to be no sleep for him this coming night.

Chapter 8

Unit 7 Brinks Mat Security Warehouse near Heathrow, 6.40am 26th November 1983

It is fair to say when life changing occurrences happen in people's lives, not only do they arrive out of the blue, but everyone responds differently, most notably victims of car accidents who start their day as they always have done yet can end it as different people. So it was to be in the case of Neil Shaw and Jim Wade. They were the two security guards to whom the responsibility of guarding the bullion in the Brinks Mat warehouse fell upon.

Just as they were fixing their first brew of the morning, the door to the reception area of the building flew open with such force the top hinges broke. They found themselves confronted by six hooded assailants who looked terrifying. The leader of the six, John Illes, marched up to Neil Shaw, whose face had turned white, and punched him so hard his nose split into two. Brian Robinson followed Mouse and assaulted Jim Wade just as violently. The third member of the gang, Bones Logan, another of Mouse's cronies from the old days, roughly ripped open Neil Shaw's trousers. He poured half the contents of a large plastic drinks bottle over his lower region, and swiftly deposited the remains of the contents over Jim Wade.

"Right," said Mouse, addressing the guards, and lighting a cigarette simultaneously. "We're going into that vault, and you know the combination lock, so get it open, now."

The smell of petrol coming from both men had put such fear into them both that their injuries sustained in

38

the assault of a few moments previously were causing them little discomfort. Mouse flicked his ash across the room towards the pair.

"Well fucking get going then" he barked. At that moment Tony Black arrived for work and walked through the door from the reception foyer right into a body blow from Bones Logan, who, despite his small frame, floored the third man immediately. Of course as Tony Black had been expecting it he had taken the precaution of adding several layers of clothing when he dressed earlier that day knowing this was where he was going to take the blow.

"Right," said Mouse, "we know you have the other half of the numbers for the combination so unless you want the petrol treatment, get to work."

Tony had not known his two colleagues were going to be doused in petrol, and showed genuine alarm as he faced them. This had been anticipated by Mouse, which not only demonstrated his sadistic nature but his cleverness as well; the fact was Mouse had instructed Bones to mix the petrol with water, so the likelihood of the guards catching fire was remote - not that in any way he was a compassionate man, he just didn't want the smell of burning flesh hampering the robbery. The other three gang members were elsewhere in the building busily de-activating the alarm systems, made considerably easier by the inside man, Tony Black. As Mouse lit another cigarette perilously close to the two guards, he was anticipating what three million pounds would look like and what denominations they would be in. The previous night he had met with Black, who had informed him that the money was indeed going to be in the vault for a few hours that morning before onward shipment. Unknown to Black, and indeed anyone present ,was the fact that five extra vans had gone in that weekend, one from Johnson Matthey the bullion merchants containing three tons of gold bars, the others were from the Diamond Trading Company carrying one thousand carats of diamonds and the other from Citibank with $250,000 of travellers cheques.

The door to the vault opened. Although Jim Wade had suffered a loss of memory initially, a lighted match close to his testicles soon restored it, and the three robbers walked in. Mouse was the first to speak:

"What the fuck?" was all that came out.

Confronting them were seventy six cardboard boxes all stuffed to the top, containing a total of 6,800 gold bars with a total weight being three tons, also two boxes of diamonds. All six robbers were now in the vault, mesmerised by the gold. Mouse's brain was racing and so was his pulse; not much flustered him, but he realised what lay before him represented the biggest haul to be taken in the history of major crime. Mouse didn't know the weight of the gold but as he lifted the first shining bar to his lips, quickly realised the transit van outside would not cope with the gold bars.

Danny Gallagher was parked discreetly round the back of Stanwell Moor; it was 6.15 am and he was confident if he was challenged he could just say he was waiting to pick up a cargo from one of the warehouses that surrounded the airport. He was contemplating being a hundred and fifty thousand pounds better off in a couple of hours, secretly hoping that Mouse had been misinformed about the haul and maybe it would be four or even five million. In any case, his hands told him he was back at work, as he continually wiped the perspiration off them. It wouldn't do for the Mouse to see him in anything other than a state of calm, and that should be anytime now. His CB radio suddenly cackled into life.

"Alpha one, alpha one, this is tango one are you

there?" he heard Mouse calling. *Great* thought Danny, *bang on time.* The call signs they had agreed on were hardly original but any radio ham listening in on the 'pilot's chit chat as they come into landing would not give it a second thought and probably not even recall hearing the message if asked; another smart move,

"Alpha one receiving what's your ETA tango one?" enquired Danny. The answer was not what he had been expecting

"Alpha one, change of plan the party's not over, get yourself round here pronto, over and out." Danny's heart missed a beat. *What the hell's happened?* he thought, as he floored the throttle. *They can't have been sussed, or Mouse wouldn't have called.* The adrenalin rushed through Danny and he felt the hairs on the back of his neck standing on end. Six and a half minutes later Danny was parked next to the transit that had arrived forty five minutes earlier with its cargo of six armed robbers. He made his way through the doors to rendezvous with the others.

His first sight was of the three security guards huddled in the corner and looking in a very bad way. His nose soon picked up the smell of petrol and human excreta as two of the guards had by now lost all self control.

"Danny, start loading these boxes now," ordered Mouse. Danny had not noticed the boxes now stacked up by the exit, and when he saw them and what they contained his eyes nearly popped out of his head.

"Yeah", said Mouse, reading Danny's mind, "It's gold, and it's worth millions. We, Danny boy, are going to be rich," he grinned.

"But what the fuck are we going to do with it, and where shall we keep it?" enquired Danny. Mouse had already worked it out.

"We are going to bury it under a ton of concrete for

five years, but as for now it goes to the original destination. Now get a move on for Christ's sake," said Mouse, wondering if he could actually sit on this for five years; after all the heat would never stop on this one.

Two hours later the seventy eight boxes of gold and diamonds had been unloaded into a lockup just off Sidcup High Street, the robbers had dispersed agreeing that they would sit tight, not contact each other, and wait for Mouse to make a decision.

As Mouse sat in the living room of his modest home in Bromley, contemplating his options, his eyes flicked to the television in the corner; the announcer was telling his audience of the breaking news that what may have been a huge robbery had taken place at Heathrow a few hours previously. He went on to say that this area had, over recent years, been dubbed Thief Row due to the large number of thefts that had taken place since the 1960s. However, he continued, the difference with this raid was that it seemed to be of particular interest to the Flying Squad of New Scotland Yard. The whole industrial state that contained the Brinks Mat warehouse had been cordoned off and the police were arriving in huge numbers.

Mouse had been thinking for several minutes, and eventually he made up his mind, one of his many associates knew all about gold and how to disguise it; he picked up the phone. He needed to move fast.

Chapter 9

Central criminal court December 3rd 1984

The central criminal court better known as the Old Bailey, sits between Holborn Circus and St Paul's Cathedral. Its former existence in the 16th century was as Newgate Gaol, a popular place in those times for the folk of London to come and watch the miscreants of the day hanged for such heinous crimes as stealing a loaf of bread. It was destroyed in the great Fire of London, and eight years later rebuilt with one side left open to the elements in the hope of preventing the spread of disease that the accused usually carried. In those days the black cap that the presiding judge would place on his head, and which preceded the handing out of the death sentence, was cheered by the watching gallery, and the betting would soon start as to how long the condemned man or woman would take between the opening of the trapdoor and the rope going taut around their neck and the final spasm indicating life had left the unfortunate person.

Nowadays the only black caps in the courtroom were those worn, usually in reverse, by family members of the accused sitting in the public gallery. All judges at the Old Bailey are addressed as "My Lord" or "My Lady," and the most senior permanent Judge is known as the Recorder of London, and his deputy has the title of Common Serjeant of London. So it was that this afternoon of December 3rd 1984, the Common Serjeant of London, Judge David Tudor, was preparing to deliver sentence on John Illes, a builder from Bromley, and Brian Robinson, a motor dealer from Sidcup, after a four week trial in which three men had stood accused of masterminding a simple but spectacular armed robbery at the Brinks Mat warehouse at Heathrow airport a year earlier. The Jury of seven women and five men had, after three nights locked in a secret location, delivered their verdict of guilty by a ten to two majority the previous day, that day being Sunday. It was the first time the court had ever been convened on a Sunday, signifying the establishment's seriousness towards the crime. The Jury had been asked to consider verdicts on the three people accused, and so when the foreman of the Jury had delivered verdicts of 'guilty' on both Robinson and Illes he was also asked how they had found Eric Logan, and he had replied, "not guilty."

The gallery burst into cries of laughter and astonishment. Eric Logan, who had spent nearly the entire previous year behind bars and who had always maintained he had been fitted up by the police, thanked the Jury and left the courthouse,. having been what seemed most reluctantly awarded several thousand pounds compensation by the Common Serjeant of London, for wrongful imprisonment. The senior police officers who had worked on the case had picked up rumours during the trial that a firm of villains from North London had been commissioned to knobble the Jury; the utmost precaution had been taken ever since the Jury were sworn in. The twelve Jury members had been under constant surveillance, likewise with their immediate families. However it was incomprehensible that Logan could be given the not guilty verdict without some skulduggery. Eric Bones Logan would be a major target for the serious crime squad from here on out, that was for sure.

Judge David Tudor Price, in his summing up of the trial, informed both defendants that the sentence must be very heavy to indicate that robberies of this kind were not worth it He said that there was no distinction between the two men, and so uttered the final words of the trial:

"You will both serve twenty five years in prison, with no remission, take them down bailiff." At their age, he may as well have put a black cap on.

Chapter 10

The investigation

Whilst Mouse was making his call to the man he figured could move the gold, Scotland Yard Flying Squad Chief Commander Frank Carter was being appointed to lead the hunt for the robbers. It was a very good choice by the big wigs from the yard, as Frank was unorthodox but got results, and he was also very knowledgeable about the criminal fraternity that inhabited the area known as greater London. He also knew that this heist could only have been undertaken by a selection of men from a pool of no more than thirty who were capable of such daring escapades.

As Frank Carter surveyed the scene of the robbery some seven hours after the gang had left, he was rapidly drawing to the conclusion that this blag was too precise to have been pulled off without inside information, certainly in his considerable experience the bigger the crime the more likely the robbers were to have an insider and this was as big as it got. As far as Frank was concerned the hunt should be for the inside man- find him, and you find the Blaggers.

During the immediate weeks that followed the raid, the great wisdom that Mouse had shown in laying low and burying the gold until the heat had died down, and generally resuming a normal life had totally evaporated. In fact almost the total opposite had occurred. Both Mouse and Brian had now left their humble abodes in South London and were both the proud owners of two estates in rural Kent paid for in cash. As if that wasn't enough to alert the Squad, Mouse had purchased two huge Rottweilers to guard his estate and named them Brinks and Matt respectively.

In the meantime, Frank Carter, head of the Sweeney, had narrowed down the list of potential suspects and both John Illes and Brian Robinson figured very highly on that list. Frank was still ruminating on the likelihood of an inside job when he got his first break; it was, as always, purely by accident that he found himself sitting in the manager's office at the Brinks Mat warehouse, waiting to go over things for the twentieth time, when the manager had been called into the warehouse, leaving him alone staring at a paperwork strewn desk. Frank, being a copper, was idly thumbing through the stacks of paper on the desk, when he picked up the three medical reports that related to the three guards who had been assaulted the morning of the robbery. All three were still on sick leave and unlikely to return in the near future, if indeed ever Casually Frank began reading the report on Tony Black; he arrived at the bottom of the report where the box labelled 'additional comments' was, and his heart skipped a beat. The box read: "The strange thing about Mr Black's injury is that whilst there is some minor bruising around the solar plexus region, the actual force used in subduing Mr Black is not conducive with that which was used on the other two; that is to say whilst Mr Shaw and Mr Wade both suffered serious injuries due to the force with which they were hit Mr Black appears to have been very lucky in only sustaining minor injuries." This was signed and dated by a Dr Samantha Pope.

Frank's intuition kicked in. *Lucky my arse*" he thought. The depot manager returned as Frank Carter put the medical report down.

"I want," he said to the manager, "every single piece of information you have on Tony Black, and I want to meet Dr Samantha Pope, and I want both these things now."

As Samantha was being summoned and the file of Tony Black being dug out of personnel, Frank had called his immediate number one, Will Peck.

"Will, I think we've got something, I want you and whoever else you need to get up the arse of Tony Black, he's one of the guards who got clobbered here and maybe he's our inside man, so right away" he commanded.

"On it Guv," came the reply.

For the next three days and nights Will Peck had been camped in the tree lined street in Crayford named Chestnut Avenue. The house occupied by Tony Black, his girlfriend Shelia Robinson, and her three children was a modest three bed semi-detached. Will had watched the comings and goings of the family, and was rapidly coming to the conclusion that this was just a normal family going about its normal business, he knew the governor was rarely wrong when it came to hunches but there was nothing out of the ordinary occurring; in fact he was figuring out how he was going to tell the boss he felt he was wasting his time. Just at that moment the passenger door of the Ford Granada Will was using that day opened and Frank Carter eased into the seat next to Will.

"What's happening Will?" asked Frank.

"Well," replied Will "To be honest, fuck all, sometimes he takes the kids to school, when he does I stay here watching the house, and Jim Mason follows him, but nothing, he always comes straight back, never a detour, nothing out of the ordinary."

"What about the phones then?" asked Frank. He had pulled a favour from one of his mates in Special Branch and they had a van parked round the corner where they were monitoring all incoming and outgoing calls-highly illegal without a magistrate's agreement and inadmissible as evidence if it ever came to court, but Frank would get round that if and when.

"Nothing there either" said Will. "The woman who's his girlfriend, Shelia Robinson, calls her mum once a day and that's about it."

"What did you just say?" Frank asked,

Will repeated that the woman rang her mum. "No, what did you say her name was?" rasped Frank.

"Shelia Robinson" was the answer.

Frank thought for a couple of seconds. "Will," he said, "It just may be a coincidence, but ten quid says it's not, that she's in fact related to Brian Robinson."

Will's stomach turned over; he knew Brian Robinson was a south London blagger, but just hadn't put two and two together, Robinson being such a common name, but that was no excuse.

"Fucking hell boss, I missed it" he said in an apologetic voice.

Frank was out of the car and twenty seconds later in the back of the Special Branch van.

"You look like the cat that got the cream," said his old mucker, from the Branch,

"Get on that phone of yours, get hold of Central Criminal Records, and get me the low down on Brian Robinson's family. I want to know if there's anyone associated with that clan by the name of Shelia," Frank said breathlessly. The man from Special Branch put the call in and made it absolutely clear this was priority one, it had to be immediately or sooner.

The three men didn't have long to wait. The man from the Branch took the call through his headphones and then set them down and looked Frank dead in the eye.

"Brian Robinson has a daughter by the name of Shelia, lives in Chestnut Avenue, with her three kids and partner Tony Black, somewhere near here I think," he said grinning from ear to ear. Frank was over the moon, he had his breakthrough, and two hours later he was at Bow Street Magistrates Court in front of the beak and a search warrant was issued.

At 6.30am the next morning two Transit Vans pulled up outside the semi-detached house in Chestnut Avenue; having obtained a warrant of entry and arrest the previous afternoon. Frank now wanted to put the fear of Christ into Tony Black. He needed to unsettle him as much as possible before the first interview that he had scheduled with him for that afternoon.

So it was that on that frosty morning that John Dawes, a resident of Chestnut Avenue for twenty years, was just leaving home for his early morning dog walk, when to his astonishment he stood mesmerised as eight burly police officers in full riot gear and a battering ram tipped out of the two vans, charged up the steps of the semi detached home opposite, smashed the door right off its hinges, piled into the private home of his neighbour and not three minutes later reappeared dragging the naked form of a man handcuffed and hooded, bundling him into the first van and then disappeared, leaving a woman and three children standing at the hole in the house where the front door had been locked and bolted a few minutes earlier. John Dawes let himself back into his own house, made a cup of tea for his wife and took it upstairs.

"There's something you ought to know about the neighbours" he said thoughtfully.

Back at Paddington Green police station, the most secure police station in England. The cells which had housed most IRA terrorists were empty apart from one man, Tony Black, whose world had suddenly fallen apart. He was out of his depth and he knew it.

Chapter 11

The Arrest

By 6.30pm that same afternoon, a written statement confessing to his part in the Brinks Mat robbery had been signed by Tony Black; it had taken the team of detectives less than four hours to break their man. Even to the police of Paddington Green and the hardened coppers of the Flying Squad, who were used to interrogating the most hardened IRA suspects, the admission had been forthcoming with surprising ease. After the first session in which Frank Carter had left Tony to ruminate on a thirty year stretch in the scrubs, Tony had spilled the beans, hoping that the police would tell the judge he had co-operated and he would then receive a lighter sentence, which had been promised by a very sincere lie from Frank Carter. As soon as the statement was signed and before the ink was dry, Frank had organised a very serious posse of armed police for the sixty mile drive to the homes of John Illes and Brian Robinson. Speed was essential as Frank was sure once the two robbers discovered Brian's brother in law was in the nick they would have it away.

John Illes was sitting in the kitchen of his Kentish mansion feeling rather pleased with himself. In the few weeks since the blag, he had managed to move the gold and it was now in the hands of various associates. He was confident none of them would turn him over. Furthermore, a company had been set up in Bristol as a gold dealership; this was currently being used as a gold smelting operation. As soon as the gold was melted down it was moved onto the scrap market and converted into cash. *Yup*, thought Mouse, *things*

51

couldn't have worked out better. The tannoy broke the silence: "John Illes; this is Commander Frank Carter of New Scotland Yard. Your house is surrounded by armed police; you and any other persons in the house are to leave by the front door immediately. You cannot run, and if you resist you will be shot."

Mouse was mortified. How could Carter be here now, he knew Carter and knew he meant business. He just retained enough presence of mind to pick up the phone to warn Brian and the rest, but the phone was dead and that said it all.

As John Illes was being shown to his new home a year later, that being A wing Her Majesties Prison Parkhurst, he was contemplating the rest of his life in this prison cell. Not in his wildest dreams could he have known that two hundred and fifty miles away a young man half way up the bleak terrain of Pen-y fan in the Brecon Beacons was going to change all that.

Chapter 11 Mike (Nine Fingers) Tobin

As Mike Tobin neared the summit of Pen-y fan he hadn't a clue who John Illes was, or that he was starting a twenty five year stretch for the Brinks Mat. He'd heard of the robbery and over a pint he had even shown begrudging admiration for the balls of the robbers, but right now he would gladly swap life on the mountain for a prison cell.

Mike Tobin joined the British Army aged eighteen. From a poor background in the North East of England, he knew life in Gateshead without qualifications or a job could only lead one way. Although uneducated, he was smart and self reliant so he had walked into the local army recruitment centre and signed up with the R.E.M.E- the Royal Electrical and Mechanical Engineers to give them their full title. Not only would

Mike get paid to see the world, well, Norway if he was lucky, but they told him at the centre he could train as a Mechanical Engineer, and he didn't know what that meant but it sounded good.

Mike took to army life like a duck to water. Based down at Bordon Camp south of Aldershot, his eager approach and natural enthusiasm made him a popular soldier within the ranks. Opposite the road from the main REME camp, and a quarter of a mile from that highway, lies an independent military barracks occupied by the Ghurkha Regiment. The rivalry between the two forces was fierce and often things got out of hand, necessitating the intervention of the Military Police.

It was after one of the regular Saturday night skirmishes with the men from the mountains of Nepal that Mike found himself in the guardhouse on three days hard labour with a rival Ghurkha as company. A few hours earlier both men had been trading blows in the local hostelry when the MPs had stormed in and grabbed the first protagonists available. Unfortunately that happened to be Mike and the Ghurkha. As the hours passed, and the two men mellowed towards each other, the little Nepalese fighter regaled Mike with stories from the Ghurkha regiment. Mike was enthralled as the Ghurkha told him of jungle warfare and how, with their diminutive frames, they fought and usually beat most adversaries and indeed, Mike realised just how vicious they were.

On the last night of incarceration the Ghurkha said to Mike: "Tell me, Mike, I've got to know you these past few days and it strikes me you want more action than the R.E.M.E. can offer. Have you ever thought about applying for the selection process of the SAS?"

Mike thought for a moment. "No I haven't, do you know how it works?" he asked.

"Well," said the Ghurkha, "Actually, yes, although we are not eligible, which is probably just as well or you English wouldn't get a look in," he laughed. "To apply is easy providing you have at least thirty nine months left to serve. Should you pass Selection Training and are between nineteen and thirty four, all you have to do is get the OK from your CO and away you go."

Mike was getting interested. "It's that easy?" he asked

The Ghurkha laughed again. "Mike we're talking about the most elite cadre of Special Forces in the world, the selection process is the most gruelling imaginable, men have died trying to obtain that badge. The pass rate varies between five and seventeen per cent; there are some fucking hard bastards that don't make the first week."

Mike's mind was made up. He was now a qualified Mechanical Engineer which he rightly figured would be an advantage. So the next morning, after he had received one hell of a bollocking for his recent escapades from his CO Major Majors, he decided to ask if the Boss would help him apply for entry into the SAS. The Major looked him straight in the eye.

"Mr Tobin," he said, "I have worked with you these past four years and you have accredited yourself admirably. The SAS are always looking for people who are above average intelligence, assertive, self-sufficient, hard to fool and not dependent on others to name just a few of the qualities required, but before all of that you have to prove you have the physical stamina to sustain weeks of untold hardship when you undergo basic selection. However, putting that to one side, you have as good a chance as anyone I've recommended before, so the answer's yes, I'll apply on your behalf and let you know Dismissed, soldier."

Six months later, months in which Mike had committed himself to the hardest training regime he could muster in addition to his normal duties, he left the comfort of Borden Camp and entered into the initial SAS recruitment process. He found himself on the bleak hillside of Pen-y fan. The fan, as it is colloquially known, comes into play in the SAS selection regime in week two. At three thousand feet the tallest and most inhospitable peak in the Brecon Beacons, this is the point where the aspiring SAS soldiers are found out. Week one saw off forty five hopeful recruits before they had even seen the fan. Mike had done OK.

Mike had seen those that had failed standing forlornly on Platform Four of Hereford station having been RTU (returned to unit), and was even more determined to make it through. On this particular day the mist had descended on the fan and Mike watched as those in front disappeared into the mire.

Mike was now carrying a fifty five pound Bergen on his back, and alone for a split second his resolve had started to waver, but just as these thoughts were taking hold he caught up with a group of men who were the lead pack. This gave him the strength to shrug off his self doubt, as they descended the Fan for the second but not the last time that day. All fears of failure left Mike, and his resolve was solid again.

As the course progressed and more and more men dropped out, Mike seemed to get stronger and stronger, and the moment of uncertainty on the misty mountain was gone and never re-appeared. The last day of basic training finally arrived, which consisted of a forty six mile endurance march known as the "Fan Dance," but having to be completed in twenty hours. It was more of a jog than a march, and carrying the obligatory fifty five pound Bergen on his back was Mike's crowning glory. Finishing third on the day, his personal road to

Damascus was complete and although there was still a long way to go, those that had made it this far were not going to fail now. That weekend, the remaining men were given the weekend off and instructed to return to Stirling Lines on the Monday for a further fourteen weeks of Continuation Training. Out of the hundred and sixty men who had started the course, thirteen left for some weekend R&R and thirteen reported back the following Monday.

On that Monday morning, the remaining thirteen men started fourteen intense weeks of Continuation Training. Mike learnt survival, escape, evasion and most significantly, extraction of prisoners and hostages from hostile environments. They were tasked on one exercise to plan and extract a prisoner from a high security prison on the British mainland, and indeed only when the operation was in the final stages of a successful conclusion was it stopped and the relevant authorities informed. The Home Office went ballistic, but points were proven. The final six weeks were spent in the jungles of Brunei, and the hardships were unimaginable- rumours abounded that the week before they arrived a large snake had eaten an Irish Ranger. The truth was that a twenty five foot Anaconda had taken him from a hide he was occupying, wrapped itself around his body, suffocated him and done just that.

Back at Stirling Lines, seven men had returned from the jungle, being the remaining existing recruits, and were waiting for the Colonel in Charge to deliver the final verdict. They didn't have to wait long before he entered the room.

"Welcome to the regiment, gentlemen" he beamed, "before I tell you of what life is going to be like in the regiment, I am going to give you your winged-dagger badges and wings, well done."

The cheer that emanated from the seven guys would have drowned a full capacity Wembley crowd and Mike was on his way.

Chapter 12

Northern Ireland - 6 Counties

The history of Northern Ireland is as complicated as the mechanics of the universe. Like all Jihads or Holy Wars no one could say when it started and similarly no one could say when it ended. Although wars based on religion never end, they develop a truce or ceasefire at best, as is the case with Northern Ireland.

When Oliver Cromwell was appointed Lord-Lieutenant of Ireland in the spring of 1649 he was tasked by Parliament to assemble a formidable force of 12,000 veterans to bring the island under British rule. During the following months, Cromwell's troops, under his orders, gave no quarter to the Catholic people who were slaughtered in cold blood. It is fair to say that the legacy of Cromwell's butchery lives on to this day in Irish folklore, making his name one of the most hated in Irish history.

Following Cromwell's introduction of the barbaric ways of the English, the most significant battle in Irish history was that which cemented the sectarianism which was already developing. The battle of the Boyne took place on July 1st 1690 and it was fought by two claimants for the English throne: James the Second, who was a Catholic, and William of Orange, a Protestant. The southern Irish, who were predominantly Catholic, were supported by James the Second, and the Northern Protestants were supported by William. Within a few hours of the battle it became clear that the forces of William would win and James beat a hasty retreat to Dublin, leaving the throne of England and the control of Ireland under the rule of the now Protestant King William of Orange. The significance of this battle of the two religious factions divided Europe at the time, and to this day tens of thousands of Orangemen march across Northern Ireland on July 12th to celebrate the great victory of the battle of the Boyne.

The final straw for the two religious factions of Ireland came on 3rd May 1921 when the British Government of the time, in their wisdom, decided to divide the country into the free state of Southern Ireland and the British run state of Northern Ireland. This essentially put the Protestants in the South and the Catholics in the North, thus creating a divided society and a period of civil conflict and disharmony followed, culminating in the Northern Ireland riots of August 1969. What followed was thirty years of bloodshed, known as "the Troubles."

Mike Tobin knew none of this history, nor if truth were told, did he care. He was stationed in the army barracks of Bessbrook Mill, the hub of counter-terrorism operations in South Armagh,bandit country as it was referred to by the inhabitants of the Mill. It overlooked the rolling hills of the county of Armagh, not far from the border of the Free State and an ideal area for the forces of the IRA to hide in and operate from. There were thirty-two SAS troopers based in these barracks, along with regular soldiers from units such as the Royal Artillery and Royal Marines. The SAS troopers kept themselves very much to themselves, not having to wear army uniform or indeed even keep clean and tidy. With their scruffy clothes and long hair they were given a wide berth by the regular soldiers, albeit the reputation of the SAS was enough for the regulars to show nothing but deference.

If the British Army had failed to learn one lesson throughout its long and chequered history, it was to never underestimate its opponents. Whenever it had engaged local indigenous people on their own soil, it had always treated them as semi- literate heathens and the IRA were considered no different. As far as the Brits were concerned, these so called freedom fighters were a bunch of potato eating paddies without a brain cell between them. Nothing could be farther from the truth; the IRA were in fact a highly sophisticated and well organised army, who had studied guerrilla warfare, both in books and on the ground, with their foot soldiers slipping on and off mainland Britain to cause havoc, and higher command training in sophisticated terrorist activities in sympathetic countries such as Libya.

The British had been in Northern Ireland long enough to know that the area of South Armagh was an ideal area for the Provo's to hide and plot in the safety of the numerous farmhouses that straddled the border between North and South. It was no coincidence that the crack troops of the SAS were stationed in Bessbrook barracks, where they could slip over the border to spy on the farms that housed the terrorists. These farms, remote and unassuming, hid various factions of the IRA; some contained specialised sniper units, a couple more were bomb factories, and another was home for a particularly notorious IRA chief of staff. It was from one of these farmhouses that one of the most spectacular achievements the IRA accomplished on the British mainland was masterminded, that being the assembly and subsequent detonation of a massive bomb which nearly brought down Canary Wharf on 9th February 1996.

The particular farm that had recently come to the attention of the British Intelligence Service sat no more than 3 miles from the border; it was occupied by three brothers and one cousin. Typical of the family connection that ran right through the borders, these four men were all killers. Trained in Syria in the art of subterfuge and stealth, they were marksmen who could assemble a deadly incendiary device from the innocent purchase of ingredients from Sainsbury's; and they were infiltrators, whose role was to cause mayhem and destruction on the British mainland. They were in the final process of planning their third sortie across the water, and were due to leave in a few days. The security measures that were in place at the farm were state of the art, a few fences and a roll of barbed wire made the farm look innocuous enough, any thing else might draw suspicion. However, strategically placed and impossible to see, were four Infra Red Heat Seeking Cameras, capable of 360 degree surveillance.These thermal imaging beams were capable of detecting any suspects which gave off body heat up to a mile away. These static cameras would pick up anything that moved, or more importantly anything that didn't move, within a one mile radius of the farm. Backing up this technology, each member of the cell carried a hand held Thermal camera. These cameras were cutting edge performance capable of allowing the user to detect any imagery in total darkness, and all supplied by the good people of Boston USA. This is where the Provo's had massive American support; most Bostonians had blood ties with Ireland somewhere down their lineage. although this support was about to take a downturn.

So it was on this cold winter's evening that the four plotters had put down the equipment they were readying for the forthcoming trip, and for the second night in succession placed the camera in the crow's nest, high up in the chestnut tree adjacent to the Dutch barn. It then picked up an object high up on the ridge that ran the length of the farm's boundary and beyond. The previous night the camera had bleeped, alerting the four protagonists to the fact something or someone was breathing on the ridge; not the first time that week, the cameras would sound off at anything from a passing fox to a low flying plane. What was now concerning the four men was the fact that in twenty four hours the living thing that the camera had been trained on since it detected life had not moved, neither had the intensity of the image, which might have suggested that an animal such as a badger was dying. If that had been the case the image would have dulled, no, something was out there, very much alive and very, very still.

"We got ourselves some company," said Dermott Donnelly, the youngest brother.

"Right," replied his older brother "let's get up there and find who or what's come to see us."

It was on this particular stormy night when it all went wrong for Mike Tobin. He was up in the hills observing the remote farmhouse just over the border, from which it was thought an IRA cell was operating, and he had been in this hide for three days and nights. Known as an OP observation point, the SAS were trained to live in these holes in the ground for days on end; you couldn't smoke, eat, or even check the magazine on the Heckler and Koch sub-machine gun you were issued with.

If you needed a crap it had to be into cling-film and then discreetly buried where you lay, to stop the unwelcome attention of rats and foxes drawing attention to your position. It was most unusual that a soldier was by himself in these circumstances, but the Commanding Officer known as the Head Shed at the barracks had felt the importance of the mission so great that secrecy was of greater importance than the increased risk of a lone soldier in hostile territory

It was just past 2am and Mike was dozing, but not enough to fail to hear the faintest sound of a twig breaking, Mike could tell the difference between an animal's nocturnal movements and a man's, and this was definitely the footfall of a man. Very slowly, Mike reached for his 9-millimeter Browning hand pistol, praying it would work if needed. He hadn't checked or oiled it for three days, and that was against the grain. Just as his hand clasped the butt of his gun he felt the cold metal of a rifle barrel pushed harshly into the nape of his neck.

"Don't move a fucking inch, you English proddy bastard" were the last words he heard before he was battered by a reign of blows that rendered him unconscious.

Several hours later Mike, who had come round, found himself in a dark dank room he could only suppose was the cellar of the farmhouse he had been watching earlier. Unfortunately, this was not the case. The gunmen that had taken him were aware that they were now under surveillance and their position had now been compromised, so they had fled with their prize twenty kilometres to the south, to a safe house that was another remote farm, heavily guarded by another IRA cell.

Mike began to assess the damage to himself, and it wasn't good. He was chained to a beam suspended from the ceiling; at least half his teeth were gone or broken, as was his nose and several of his ribs. His head was covered with a hood and his toes had been broken to stop him running (not that there was much likelihood of that at this precise moment). To make matters worse, Mike had no idea if his capture would have been noticed, as he wasn't due to make contact with his handler for another five days. What he would have dearly liked to know, was whether a miniature tracking device had been slipped into the last meal he ate back at the barracks; it was considered by the hierarchy that if a trooper was captured and knew he was carrying a tracker, and admitted such a thing under extreme torture, he would probably be eliminated immediately. Mike hoped his tracker had not yet passed through him. The only positive angle Mike could find was that he was still alive, but even that gave him cold comfort as he was only too aware what the IRA did to special forces personnel if they were unlucky enough to get captured.

Several hours later, Mike heard the bolts of the door being drawn and steeled himself for what was inevitably going to be a slow and extremely painful execution. The hood was ripped off his head, not a good sign as the people that held him were not afraid of showing their faces, meaning there would be no future for him and no identification parades.

"Well, well, just look what we caught ourselves here," said the man now nose to nose with Mike. Mike was looking into the eyes of a psychopathic maniac grinning like a Cheshire cat. The IRA chief of staff for Armagh stood six and a half feet tall, with a great swath of red hair and a spider's web tattoo covering his face. He could put the fear of Christ up any man on earth.

"Now Mr. SAS man, I'm not going to fuck about," he said in a deep Irish accent, " I'm not going to tell you can make it easy for yourself, you can't, but if you want to tell us all about yourself you can, but over the next few days we are going to cut you into small pieces, but ever so slowly so you don't bleed to death on us, and then we're going to post them to your mates back at Bessbrook, and just for good measure we'll send some nice photos to Hereford, you fucking English pig."

With that the Irish giant spat into Mike's face, head butted him with the force of an express train on his broken nose, replaced the hood and left the room. For a few seconds back on the Fan, Mike had briefly glimpsed the feeling of failure, this time all the resolve in the world couldn't allay the sinking feeling in his stomach; he thought about his life and passing the training regime back at Hereford, all to end in a shithole in the arse end of a bog in Ireland. What he was about to go through was unthinkable a few days earlier.Three days later, semi-conscious and lying in his own excrement, they came for him, the red-haired giant and two disciples.

"Now you're well and truly rested we can begin," said the giant as the two henchmen delivered vicious kicks into Mike's groin. They unshackled him and dragged him up two flights of stairs to a kitchen area, where they shoved him into a wooden chair, tied him securely and removed the hood which had become part of Mike in recent days. As Mike tried to focus through the one good eye he had left, he suddenly noticed on the chair directly in front of him was a man not dissimilar to himself, with a broken face tied to a chair. Both men looked at each other in abject astonishment. Spiderman laughed.

"We like to do things in twos round here," he spat. "You two bastards can have the pleasure of watching each other have your fingers cut off, then your ears, then your toes, then your eyes then your bollocks, but I think your balls can come off with the blow torch, just for a bit of variety. Allow me to introduce you to each other .Mr SAS man, meet Mr Parachute Regiment man." Both men starred at each other incredulously. The Para, Toby Wakefield, had a couple of weeks earlier been on patrol, discreetly observing an official IRA funeral. As the procession of hooded terrorists and mourners had been making their way down the Falls Road in Belfast, Toby just happened to stray past an alleyway where he lingered for a split second too long. Out of the depths of the alley, an opportunist snatch squad of republicans grabbed him from behind and disappeared behind one of the many doorways that littered the alley. By the time Toby's mates had realised he was missing, and had ripped every door in the street of their hinges, Toby was in the republic and awaiting his fate.

The stench from the two men in one room was almost unbearable but the three IRA men, all sadists, were relishing the sport they were about to undertake, and didn't appear to notice anything untoward.

"Right, lets get started" said the red -haired man "Either of you two got anything to say?" he inquired of Mike and Toby. Neither man said a word, if anything they were taking some solace in each other's predicament. One of the tattooed man's disciples opened a cupboard under the sink and produced a set of industrial bolt croppers, he looked at the two prisoners and flipped a coin, heads SAS first, tails the Para. The other two found this highly amusing. The coin landed and tails showed. Mike had kind of hoped he'd be first , purely for selfish reasons, to get it over with and not witness what he was about to receive.

With no more talk the Irishman who had not yet spoken named Declan spread Toby's hand open and selected the first finger of his left hand, staring into his eyes he secured the tool around the base of Toby's little finger and gradually tightened his grip. As the finger fell to the floor Toby thankfully passed out and didn't give the fenian bastards the satisfaction of screaming. Pleased with his work, the IRA man let the enormity of the moment register with Mike and asked him one time: "Anything to say now?"

Mike thought for a moment; if he started talking could he put off the dreadful events that were unfolding? He concluded not, and just looked into the ceiling. The man named Declan was pleased there was to be no delay, not at this early stage anyhow. *When these two bastards see the blow torch they'll be singing for their lives then,* he thought. He took Mike's left hand, selected the little finger, looked into Mike's eyes, placed the cutter round the base, exerted just enough pressure to ensure maximum pain and squeezed.

As Mikes finger came off, the world caved in; at first Mike thought it was the sensation of his amputation, but quickly realised salvation had come. The windows flew through the kitchen, as did the door; simultaneously three CS gas canisters burst open, the main door caught Spiderman full in the chest but before he hit the deck six bullets from an MP5 sub-machine gun had entered his gut, and he was dead before the floor greeted him The other two IRA men fared no better. Declan took twenty two bullets through the head and torso, and the remaining terrorist was cut in half by the automatic fire of the MP5.

Four hours later Mike and Toby were in the field hospital at Bessbrook barracks. Both had identical bandages on their respective left hands. Word had got round of their ordeal, and even for the respectful soldiers inhabiting the barracks, people were finding excuses to come and see the two heroes, as they were now being labelled.

The next morning a land rover pulled up alongside the hospital, and a colonel from the Parachute Regiment entered.

"Morning, Toby." he said "Let's get you home where you belong, don't want you mixing with this lot any more than you have to, they will get you into trouble if you're not careful."

Toby looked at Mike. "Not even time for a beer then," he said.

"Doesn't look like it," replied Mike, "but mark my words, when we next meet, the first ones on me."

Little did he know there would be a next time, and little did he know the circumstances under which that beer would be drunk.

From that day on Mike Tobin became known amongst the elite cadre of Special Forces, the SAS, as Nine Fingers, quickly abbreviated to Nine. He had won his spurs.

Chapter 13

Brinks Mat- the aftermath

Danny Gallagher sat in the living room of his modest but comfortable home in the village of Goudhurst, Kent. He had a lot on his mind and sleep was not going to come easy that night. Tomorrow morning he was going to drive to the affluent Hertfordshire town of Harpenden, where he was to rendezvous with three other conspirators, and at precisely 11.45am they intended to relieve the St. Albans branch of Barclays Bank of what he had calculated to be several hundred thousand pounds. By 4pm he was due on the Eurostar from Folkestone to Paris, and then booked on the 9pm flight out of Charles de Gaulle bound for Marrakesh, where he intended to stay for three months until the heat of the blag had died down. This was never going to be a payday to match the Brinks Mat but even so it would yield enough for Danny to escape forever. The morning's raid had been planned with meticulous precision and his accomplices chosen with the utmost caution. Danny's brother Sammy was already ensconced in the Glen Eagles Hotel, Harpenden High Street, booked in under an assumed name. He looked every part the travelling businessman and this was his first blag since Danny had visited his pub on the Costa Del Sol all those years ago. Sammy's business on the Costa del crime had nosedived in recent years as the criminal fraternity had become bored with Spain and sought more glamorous hidey holes in the Caribbean and South America. Like Danny, Sammy was committed to one last blag and then wanted to disappear for good.

This was, however, not what Danny was

contemplating as he sat alone staring into space. His thoughts were focused on the years since the incarceration of John Illes and Brian Robinson. He had evaded capture following their arrest, but never a day had passed without him looking over his shoulder, either for the old bill to come calling, or worse, an assassin's bullet in the back of the neck. Immediately after the robbery, it became clear that the bullion was not going to be as easy to move as Mouse had first thought. No-one within the immediate circle of the robber's acquaintances had any experience of dealing with gold, indeed up until then armed robbery had been a strictly cash only business, and so the call had gone out far and wide for help. The call that the Mouse had made all those years ago had been to a shadowy figure in London's underworld, to a man known as The Fox. For thirty years The Fox had been one of the senior figures in British organised crime and Mouse figured if anybody could help it would be The Fox. Mouse was right, The Fox was able to contact two of London's most notorious gangs, to help move the gold. One accepted, and one wisely declined, figuring anyone touching the bars would get seriously burned. Thus the gold found itself being distributed through a network of villains, some of which were known to Mouse, and some not, but as long as Mouse kept a stranglehold of the situation it was the best he could do.

Following the arrest of Mouse and Brian Robinson, things changed. The initial divvy up of the bullion had occurred ten days before the arrest of Mouse, that is to say, the gold which was handed out was for safekeeping rather than personal usage. With Bones Logan and Herbie Sparks being entrusted with a thousand bars each, Danny also got a thousand bars and the two Petermen a thousand between them. The remainder was split between Mouse, Danny, and Brian

Robinson. When news of the arrests broke, panic set in amongst the initial team. Would Mouse sing to save his arse? No-one could say, but everyone knew he would effectively be facing a life sentence if found guilty and under those circumstances, who wouldn't.

Ironically the two Petermen were the first to crack; they figured Mouse would be away for such a long stretch that he was effectively rendered harmless, and in any case would have more on his mind coping with the rest of his life in the shovel than to worry about his gold. They both knew many villains who they figured would take the gold for cash; they could then disappear back into the world at large never to be heard of again. So within three days of Mouse's capture, a white Hertz rental van pulled off the highway between The Wake Arms and Theydon Bois, an area known as Epping Forest, and the two safebreakers entered the forest, went to the spot where their entrusted cargo was buried, dug it up, loaded the van and hit the road north to Scotland.

Twenty hours later in a derelict warehouse in Glasgow's East End, the exchange took place. The scene could have been taken from a hundred gangster movies, with the two Petermen in one corner and the Glasgow Mafia, totalling six men and all heavily tooled up in another. Whilst the Englishmen were extremely vulnerable, they had worked with these Glaswegian hoodlums in the past, so were fairly confident they wouldn't get rolled over. As it happened they had nothing to fear; the transaction completed, they left Glasgow 800k richer and the boys from Barlinnie returned to their haunts with a thousand gold bars valued by Johnson Matthey at 3.8 million pounds. All happy then, apart of course from prisoner 134859 Illes of her Majesties Prison Parkhurst.

It took just two weeks for word of the betrayal to

reach A wing. John Illes was being turned over by those he trusted and if he didn't send a message out very quickly he knew the empire would collapse and there would be nothing left of the loot within six months, let alone when he got out.

Mouse realised he had to get out of jail sooner rather than later, no matter what the cost. He acted with as much haste as the judicial system would allow, and within twenty four hours he was sitting in the Governor's office facing Chief Superintendant Frank Carter.

"Well, here I am, John" said the Sweeney boss. "What is you want?" he asked, pretty sure he had already guessed,

Mouse gritted his teeth. "I want to turn Queen's" he said "I'll give you everyone, but I want out, I want out now, and I need £100,000 grand to get lost."

Frank Carter stared at Mouse, and shook his head slowly.

"Honour amongst thieves is it then, John?" he smirked. "Let me tell you" he continued, "the return of Jesus Christ is more likely to happen than you getting out of here. You knock off twenty six million quid and then think you can grass up a few mates and get off the hook! I don't think so. Listen, your assets are about to be seized, you are soon going back to the Bailey to be ordered to pay back the twenty six million, that's with a capital M. Should you ever be released, or if you try to contact me again. I won't come. Warden, take this trash back to his cell."

The door slammed shut leaving Mouse stunned and very alone.

Word soon started to filter through the underworld that John Illes had been ripped off, and that the gold was being held by at least a dozen crooks, and the heat was intense. Danny Gallagher had been raided twice, nothing found, but the old bill had got their message across: the heat wouldn't stop until the gold was found and the remaining robbers reunited with Mouse.

Oddly enough, just like the two safecrackers but without knowing it, Danny had also buried his stash in Epping Forest. If future generations ever dug up the Forest they would assume it was some ancient burial ground, what with all the bodies from gangland wars deposited there, and the hidden booty from blags where the villains for one reason or another never got back to claim their ill-gotten gains. Danny, however, being the shrewd fellow he was, had never set foot in Essex since he hid his bars; furthermore until someone told him John Illes was dead he was not about to let greed jeopardise his own life.

Six months passed. The two safecrackers had long gone, and Eric Logan and Herbie Sparks found themselves one evening sitting in the garden of the Cricketers public house just off Bromley common. Eric was the first to broach the subject.

"Herbie," he said, out of earshot of the surrounding families enjoying some early spring sun. "Mouse isn't coming out, the other two have sold their share and fucked off, we can wait till the cows come home, or we can offload our bit and do the same."

Herbie replied, "That's all well and good, but even in stir Mouse is not going to sit back and let us steal his gold. I've already heard a whisper that there's a contract out for Flint and Batter, the Petermen"

"Well I say we take a chance," stated Bones. "I know who the bloke is in Hatton Garden who's been taking the stuff, and I know that they've set up a hooky company down in Bristol to smelt it down. If we just sit on this stuff for the next twenty years we'll probably get sussed in any case, so we've nothing to lose."

"Apart from our lives," observed Herbie.

73

"Well, how about I go to Hatton Garden, make a couple of enquiries and then make a decision?" asked Eric.

"Agreed," was Herbie's hesitant response.

It was soon after this clandestine meeting that Danny received his summons. It came in the form of an official envelope, and although Danny knew the contents he still felt desperate. The envelope contained a Visiting Order from Her Majesties Prison Parkhurst, with Danny's name on. He was requested to visit John Illes, currently holidaying on the he Isle Of Wight, and the invitation was for the following Tuesday. This was the first word Danny had heard from Mouse since the arrest, and he had been just starting to hope Mouse had resigned himself to his fate, but obviously this was not the case, and ominously Mouse was not the type of bloke to send out a Visiting Order because he was lonely. So it was with trepidation that Danny travelled to the Island that next Tuesday. He was sitting in the visitor's room, feeling sick with the smell of the prison that all old lags hated so much, when Mouse was escorted in. In all fairness, Mouse didn't look too bad - unusually for prison life he hadn't lost weight and he was yet to develop the dead eyes so common with lifers. After the usual pleasantries, Mouse spoke in a lowered tone:

"Danny, I'm being burnt. Word is the two safecrackers have already sold the gold they were holding for me. Logan and Sparks have contacted the Hatton Garden contact and three of the other guys who you don't know have suddenly become very wealthy. What do you know? What have you heard?"

Danny replied, "It's true, I know the gold's on the move because half the fucking country is wearing it. I heard rumours about the sale of the stuff to the sweats, but nothing about Bones or Herbie jacking it in."

Danny could only tell the truth, he was still sitting on his pile and at this particular point very thankful he hadn't touched it. However, he wasn't expecting what came next.

"Listen to me very carefully," said Mouse "I have no choice here, and I'm sorry it's you Danny, but you're the only one I trust."

That was a compliment Danny didn't want to hear, and he dreaded the next words.

"So what you have to do," Mouse whispered, "is have those bastards dealt with, and by that I mean permanently."

"Who exactly are we talking about here?" asked Danny, his throat dry as the Sahara desert.

"The fucking lot of them," snarled Mouse," when you leave here today that screw by the window will escort you out, he will slip you a piece of paper with the names of four people, the first three are the thieving bastards who stole my gold, which you don't know, and the fourth is the man you need to contact who will deal with them."

"So you want me to arrange a hit on these three guys?" Danny asked.

"Seven of the bastards in total" replied Mouse.

Danny left the prison feeling faint with fear; he had done some bad things in his time but he had just unwittingly agreed to assist in the murder of seven men. Two of them, Eric and Herbie, he could almost call friends. Momentarily he considered leaving the gold in Epping Forest and getting the hell out of Blighty for good, but he knew this ball was rolling and if he did that Mouse would assume he had also ripped him off and that would make him number eight. No, he would organise the hitman, then organise himself one last job,and leave Mouse's money exactly where it was and get well and truly lost.

Now, on the eve of the final chapter of this saga, Danny was a lot happier than he had been that day he walked out of the prison. Several years had passed; there had been no comebacks on the murders of those that had double- crossed Mouse, and in all fairness very little heat from the old bill at all regarding the violent end of seven turncoats. 'Good riddance' was the unofficial stance the Met took when villains inevitably turned on themselves. Danny had been to see Mouse the previous week .He had told Mouse his plans, and he had explained that the gold was still buried in Epping Forrest and that if Mouse was ever released, or needed access, Danny would ensure he was available to retrieve it. Danny was fearful that Mouse would think he was lying and making off with the swag, but Mouse trusted him and granted him absolution. Mouse had thanked Danny and wished him luck for his imminent escapade. All was well.

Danny's thoughts drifted back to the meeting with the unnamed American, whose number he had been given by the bent warden. He had known that when he made the call he would now become an accessory to murder, and he reconsidered his options hoping there was another solution, but soon realised when he had made that commitment back in his brother's bar to team up with Mouse, that his bridges had been burnt. He made the call.

No details were discussed on the phone; the meet was arranged for the following day at the entrance to Brighton Pier.

Danny was told to carry a small bunch of flowers and he would be contacted. As hard as Danny was, he was shitting himself; this was so far out of his league his mind was racing. This could go tits up, what if the would -be assassin was the filth? What if the assassin was some Mafiosi type who would do the hits then rub him out? As he stood there pondering the outcome, a very ordinary, slim built man walked past and then turned in surprise, "My God, its Danny Gallagher" said the man with an American accent "it must be 15 years."

Danny was just about to tell the stranger to fuck off when it dawned on him this was the meet, and that this was the man who was going to murder the seven guys, who had once been part of, the team that Danny had worked with. Hell's Teeth, thought Danny, he looked so ordinary. Both men instantaneously stretched out their left hands, shook and slapped each other on the back, as old friends might. Danny was surprised that the man in front of him was so unassuming and nothing like the person he had imagined, but of course Mouse always insisted on the best so this guy was hardly likely to have any impediments which would draw attention to him. Danny felt better, and the American suggested they walk along the sea front and catch up on the lost years. As soon as they were out of earshot the American spoke:

"Right, Danny, I need names, locations if possible but not essential, a time frame, and you mentioned on the phone you had more than one car for sale, how many?"

"Seven" replied Danny.

The American blew through his teeth. "Jesus" he said.

Danny then explained the reasons for the multiple executions, including the fact that the two safe crackers were currently in unknown areas of the world didn't appear to worry the American, who spoke very precisely:

"Ok, then here's the deal, this is a huge job, number one, these people will have to be taken out over a period of time, probably at six monthly intervals at best, or the British police will start making connections.

Number two, before each hit; I want fifty percent of the fee up front. When the job is done I will send you proof, and when you receive that proof, no more than five days later I want the balance of the money paid into the account that will accompany the evidence of the hit. Do you foresee any problems so far?"

Danny swallowed. Was he really hearing this?

"This is our first and last meeting" the American hitman continued. "The payment is fifty big ones for each of the guys whose whereabouts you give me, and a hundred large for the two who are on the run, and lastly in which order would you like me to start?"

Danny couldn't believe that in ten minutes he had just signed the death warrant of seven men. He could see each of their faces clearly in his mind, and he thought about the last question.

"Right," he replied, "I agree to everything you've said, you had best take the guys out who were on the initial job first, that will get the message out that no one fucks with Mouse and gets away with it."

"Good thinking," replied the American assassin. The ten minutes he had allowed himself to spend with his client were up.

"It was lovely bumping into you after all these years, now I've got to hit the road, so get those lovely flowers to Madge before they wilt" he said, and with that he was gone, leaving Danny wondering how the anonymous American had known his wife's name. He shuddered, and not because of the cold Brighton air, he looked around and he was on his own.

Six weeks later, just as Danny was starting to convince himself it had all been a bad dream, he received his first instructions: to deposit twenty-five thousand in a bank account in Pennsylvania, USA.

Eric Logan had done well, he now owned a pub and a thriving mini-cab business, and he was convinced his future was secure; there had been no fallout over his treachery and he was on the up, with two legitimate businesses to his name. The world was all well with him as he locked up his office on the last night of his life, and he didn't even see the lone gunman who walked up behind him and fired two bullets into the back of his neck, leaving his brains pebble dashing the front door of his newly painted office.

The next letter Danny got was a cutting from the London Evening Standard describing the shooting of a South London businessman, with known underworld connections. The letter also contained the name and account number of a bank in Oregon, USA. Danny didn't wait five days to pay the money into the American bank, he did it that afternoon.

Herbie Sparks had panicked- word had spread like wildfire after Bones Logan's untimely death, that retribution was coming for those that had been stupid enough to think Mouse was impotent in his prison cell. Herbie hightailed it out of London and relocated to the wilds of Derbyshire; he took over the local Post Office, assumed a new identity and began to sleep again at nights. It was not enough. As he sat in the saloon bar of his now local pub six months later, at last starting to feel a little easier, a motorcyclist walked into the pub and asked if there was a Mr Sparks in tonight. Herbie, caught totally unaware, replied "That's me, mate," upon which the black clad gunman pulled out a pistol, shot Herbie between the eyes twice, and marched briskly out, leaving the yokels stunned and terrified.

Danny received the newspaper cutting from the Derbyshire Evening Post two days later. 'Innocent drinker murdered in sleepy village pub, publican in state of shock', was what he read; also in the letter was the name of a bank account in Lyon, Southern France.

And so the killing continued, until all seven had

been snuffed out. Danny wondered if his turn would come. Although he had stayed loyal to Mouse, probably out of fear for his life, he couldn't be sure, and so here he was. In a few hours he would be out of it for good. He slipped into a fitful doze for what remained of the night.

Chapter 14

The Bank Robbery

At 5.30am the next morning Danny rose from his bed, now fully focused on the day ahead. Both he and Madge had decided she should open up the stall as normal. When the police started taking statements from all those in the vicinity of the raid it might look suspicious if their stall was not functioning. As always, Madge was already awake and busying herself. They quickly covered the plans of the day and the rendezvous at Maidstone for the hundredth time and said their goodbyes. Madge took the van, and headed north for the Nine Elms fruit and veg market and Danny took Madge's five year old Honda, less conspicuous than the 750 series BMW that he had recently taken charge of. Danny's accomplices were three in number. His brother Sammy was going in first, armed with a sawn off shotgun, his brief was to blast open the security door that separated the staff from the public, and get them all on the ground before anyone hit the panic button. Providing the panic button wasn't hit, they had estimated they had five minutes before the general alarm was raised. If some lucky bastard got to the button they had three minutes. Danny, over the period of time he had been watching the bank and calling in with regular deposits, had worked his timing out to a second; if everyone did exactly as they should, they could be in and out in two and a half minutes, worst case scenario they could do the bank if the panic button was hit. The other two blaggers were faces Danny knew and trusted, unusually for London gangs, who kept themselves to themselves, territorially at least, the two Danny had chosen were Essex lads who ran a scrap business down the A13. Danny felt he needed new blood on this one, there was too much history south of the water, and furthermore once it was over and everyone had assumed their normal lives, these boys lived and operated very close to Epping Forrest, which meant they might prove useful at a later date. Neither of them knew any of the history of the Brinks Mat apart from what the papers trawled up every so often.

Like all East End villains, Ugly Dave Johnson and Tommy "the fly" Payne had their roots going back to the heyday of East End crime when the Krays and Richardson's ruled the roost. Ugly Dave and the Fly were part of this folklore, some true some not, what was true was that Dave Johnson had acquired the additional forename Ugly following a brutal beating, which necessitated sixty stitches to his face, from officers of the West End Vice Squad following his refusal to grass up a couple of his mates who were holding a large quantity of smack, which the Vice Squad boys required.

As is the code of villainy, a man who takes a good hiding is classified as all right, and his reputation is secured. Tommy Payne earned his moniker shortly after him and Ugly moved to the scrap yard. Tommy, a fearless bastard, decided to rip off the Essex pikies with a series of cons involving a number of top end motors, and the pikies fell for the ruse, mainly because they considered themselves untouchable, certainly anybody with a modicum of respect for their lives would steer well clear of these Irish tinkers. So the pikies named Tommy 'the fly', like the fly on the end of a line to tempt and cheat the great trout in the Liffey. They did of course, after discovering they had been conned, also deliver one hell of a beating to the East End wide boy, and all parties lived in a state of truce thereafter.

Six months previously, Danny Gallagher had come calling to the scrap yard down the A13 with a proposition. There was a bank, in a nice quite town in Hertfordshire waiting to be robbed. Danny needed two more for the team, and he needed men who could put the fear of Christ up the arses of the staff and customers of the bank, furthermore he needed a small getaway van, ideally with a refitted engine that could deliver in excess of two hundred horses. He needed tooling up, three sawn off shotguns, three hand guns and three CS gas canisters to set off as they left the bank. Were they interested, he asked.

"Has David Attenborough got a fucking Passport?" replied Ugly. "Course we're interested."

The payout was agreed, all equal four ways, and the Essex boys could even take the swag back to the yard immediately after the job, probably best as there are a million places to hide illicit goods in a scrap yard, and most illicit goods had already been transported through that particular scrap yard on the A13.

As dawn broke on the morning of the robbery, the big black gates of the scrap yard opened and two motors pulled out, a cut and shut Mercedes S class and a white Renault 35cwt van. Both had false number plates, one was coming back tonight, and one wasn't. In the back of the Renault were four large canvas sports bags, and they would also be returning tonight but by then they would be full of the cash that was currently being loaded into the armoured van that was due to deliver it to St. Albans that morning. Under the bags were the shooters that Danny had ordered, as well as two canisters of CS gas, and two canisters of Mustard gas. The provider of the assorted weapons, known aptly as the quartermaster, had had great difficulty getting the gas and had warned the boys that the Mustard gas was only to be used if they were in deep shit.

The Essex boys were soon making their way through the back lanes to Harlow, and then onward to Borehamwood, with the Fly behind the wheel of the van and Ugly Dave in the Merc.

Sammy Gallagher was also on the move, having checked out of the Gleneagles hotel, he was returning his hired car to the Hertz garage opposite Luton Broadway station. He checked his watch, dead on time, he didn't want to be hanging around either on the platform at Luton or outside the station at Borehamwood. As far as Sammy was concerned, the job was underway right now, and that meant precision timing from this moment on.

In the meantime, Danny had had an uneventful journey up from Kent, and he had parked Madge's car in Arden Grove, Harpenden. This was an unrestricted street near the town centre and station where many commuters took advantage of the free all day parking, and no one would be any the wiser. Danny made his way round to the station, stopping to glance in the local estate agent's windows, not to check out local house prices but to be comfortable he wasn't being watched. At exactly 9.28am the Bedford to St Pancras slow train, stopping at all stations, pulled into Luton Broadway and Sammy Gallagher stepped on board carrying that day's Daily Telegraph and nothing else. All the possessions he had had during his stay at the Gleneagles had been parcelled up and posted home the night before; the years of thieving had taught Sammy and the rest that when you were going to undertake a criminal activity, you travelled light and with no identification that could inadvertently be left at the scene of a crime.

At 9.54am the slow train to St Pancras pulled up at platform 3 Harpenden Rail Station. Danny Gallagher stepped on board, acknowledged his brother with an upward movement of his thumb, took a seat further down the carriage and settled down. At 10.06 the train, heading towards St Pancras at a snail's pace, pulled into St. Albans City station. Among the passengers boarding was a deeply scarred man from a scrap yard down the A13. He made eye contact with his two co-conspirators, and took a seat between the two brothers.

Half an hour earlier, Ugly Johnson had arrived in St. Albans in the untraceable Merc S class He had driven to an area just outside the city centre known as Bernard's Heath, north of the city but only a couple of minutes drive, and the ideal spot to switch motors after the blag, unload the cash from the Renault and leave Danny to dump the van and shooters in Harpenden. Sammy and the two Essex boys would then hit the motorway and be back in the safety of the scrap yard in an hour. There were plenty of dog walkers on the Heath that morning and the Merc would not draw attention to itself for the short time it was staying.

At 10.25 the souped up Renault van pulled into the parking lot of Borehamwood station and waited for the slow train to St Pancras. Three minutes later the train pulled in, dead on time. Danny, Sammy, and Ugly Johnson were the last to alight, taking their time and letting the passengers that also disembarked at Borehamwood leave the train first. Without a word Danny, Ugly and Sammy joined up and walked briskly to the waiting van. They had practised this on at least three occasions; they knew the exact location of the van, away from the security of the CCTV, not that anyone would be looking for these robbers at Borehamwood railway station, but still a worthwhile precaution. The back doors were open and Danny and Sammy climbed into the back, Ugly into the front.

"Ready then," said The Fly to the two brothers.

"As ready as we'll ever be" came the stock reply. Danny and Sammy rummaged through the bags on the floor; both quickly found what they were seeking,

"So," enquired Danny "these shotguns, have all possible means of identification been removed?"

"Clean as a whistle" replied The Fly.

"And how about the van?" asked Sammy.

"The same" came the answer.

The plan was that after the blag the van was going to be dumped down a small bridleway which Danny had identified near Harpenden High Street. He would torch the van, and then return to his car empty handed, and head off to Maidstone meet up with Madge and get off to Paris. The other three would be dropped in Bernard's Heath just off St. Albans city centre, where Dave Johnson had left the Merc. Torching the van was as much a diversionary tactic as destroying the evidence; all the men were wearing protective clothing head to foot and there would be no evidence left in or on the van to associate them with the robbery, even if for some reason Danny could not burn the van. They were all professionals after all.

At 11.30am the white Renault van cruised north up St Peter's Street, the main through route of St Albans. As the van drew up to the lights for pedestrians to cross, all eyes in the van were focused on the event occurring outside Barclays Bank, to their immediate right. A black armoured vehicle was stationary outside the bank and a heavily clad guard was carrying large boxes of money into the premises. The van proceeded up the high street where it turned left and left again to position itself in a small lay-by approximately fifty meters from the main bank entrance.

"All ready?" asked Danny, the other three all replied in the affirmative. Normally Danny would have been the wheels man, but on this occasion there was an outside possibility that he might be recognised sitting in the van, so Tommy Payne stayed where he was behind the wheel and the other three jumped out, with the shotguns under their jackets and balaclavas ready to go on as soon as they stormed into the bank. Sammy was first in, immediately followed by Ugly Dave. Danny stood by the door, Sammy let one barrel off into the ceiling, and the next discharge from the sawn off blew the door between the public and the staff access off its hinges.

"Every fucker down now" he barked.

The staff dropped to the floor, all apart from the Manager who started to protest. The butt of Sammy's shotgun was rammed into his face, teeth and blood spewed everywhere and the Manager fell to the floor; the four members of the public who were unlucky enough to be in the bank at the time all dropped to the ground. Sammy stood over the bank staff whilst Ugly Dave ran behind him through the gap where the door had been and looked for the recent delivery. Just as Danny had said, the boxes were now open and the cash being transferred to the vault; complacency had set in over the years at this bank and now they were going to pay for it - if the manager ever recovered from his violent assault he would probably lose his job, but that was the least of his worries at the moment. Sammy wasn't sure if the alarm button had been hit- he looked to the door for the signal from Danny, who opened and closed his left hand three times. This was the agreed sign that fifty five seconds had elapsed since they entered, and they were on time. Ugly Dave busied himself with filling the canvas bags they had brought, the boxes were emptied and two bags stuffed with money. Dave first, then Sammy, made their way to where Danny was standing, having emptied the cash boxes in a further forty five seconds. Nothing was said. Danny flipped the tops off the two gas canisters, rolled them across the floor of the bank, and the three men fled out of the ramshackled building to the waiting van. They left behind a scene of total carnage, screams were coming from the bank and the passerby's who were witnessing the raid were fleeing as if a bomb had been detonated.

Dave, Danny and Sammy jumped into the back of the van and Tommy Payne gunned it away from the scene. Three minutes later, the Renault van pulled up on Bernard's Heath, a few meters from the parked S class. Still not a word was said. They had rehearsed these moments so many times nothing needed to be, every second from here on out was vital. The overalls they had worn were now discarded in the back of the van, as were the shotguns. The hand guns were kept in case things went belly up and there had to be a shoot out, of which they were all prepared and capable. Danny gave his gun to Sammy, who was now going to be most at risk in the next thirty minutes or so. The three men who were travelling back to Essex got into the Mercedes leaving Danny to dump the van as planned, pick up his own motor and hit the road. The Merc, after no more than a minute since they had arrived in the van, pulled onto the main road and headed for the ring road. The plan was, if all had gone according to schedule, the Merc would head up to the M1 at Hemel Hempstead before heading south. The gang had figured that all motorway slip roads around St. Albans would be shut, and if the old bill were really on the ball this would be within thirty minutes of the time they left the bank. They had plenty of time, so no breaking speed limits on the way to Hemel; they were as good as home and dry.

This, however, was not the case for Danny; he still had to get shot of the van, which meant another fifteen minutes in the Renault. As he passed the Ancient Briton Public house on his way to Harpenden, three police vehicles came screaming in the opposite direction. Danny's heart was racing, did they know a Renault van was the getaway vehicle, he would find out in a few seconds, the squad cars drew level and then passed. Danny checked his mirror; if he saw them brake he was prepared to outrun them, and he had planned where he could ditch the van if chased, and the Essex boys had done a good job with the engine, so if the worst came to the worst he was still confident of his escape. The police cars flew by, straight through the red lights at the pub and were gone. Danny was mightily relieved; he was now entering the last phase.

Five minutes later Danny was reversing the van into the small pull in up the track he had identified not far from his parked car, but remote enough to torch the van and not be seen. As Danny got out of the driver's door, preparing to burn the Renault, a tractor appeared coming from the top of the lane towards him. Fuck it, were Danny's first thoughts. To make matters worse, the driver pulled up about 100 meters from where Danny was parked. Danny looked and could just make out that the driver was pouring himself a cup of coffee from a flask, and opening a package of tin foil. Unbelievable, thought Danny, he's having his fucking lunch. Danny had to think fast; if he torched the van the man might have a phone or radio and call the fire brigade, or even worse the police, or both- he would definitely notice Danny whatever. If Danny left the van there was a chance the tractor driver might assume the van was owned by a dog walker and ignore it. Danny considered what incriminating evidence was in the van, well the shooters for starters. However, they had considered this option, and the van was untraceable and everything was wiped clean. With a bit of luck, the van might not cause suspicion until Danny was clear of England. He made his decision; he locked the van, threw the keys into the hedge and walked. It was the wrong decision.

Down in Harpenden High Street, PC Dave Evans was on patrol. His brief that morning from the duty Sergeant was to walk the town centre, make sure traffic was flowing, check the occasional car for tax etc: in general, be seen by the good burghers of Harpenden as a police presence. Really a day as ordinary as the last fifty had been; in fact in the last year, PC Dave Evans had detained one shoplifter from Sainsbury's. He had been alerted by a nosy shopper, who had watched the thief nick a bottle of scotch from the wine department, and then collared the policeman along the high street and pointed him out. That had been his sum total of arrests; he was beginning to wonder if policing was all it was made out to be.

As he made his way to the station, he glanced at the five year old Honda parked alongside the other commuter cars. The tax was a couple of days overdue, nothing remarkable really but nonetheless it constituted a motoring offence.. PC Evans wasn't even sure if he should take down the number- maybe the occupant was already at the post office taxing it now, maybe he should find a traffic warden and ask them to keep an eye on it, he couldn't really justify waiting for God knows how long for the owner to return, so he walked on. Just as he reached the corner to turn for the railway station, he looked back and there was a man unlocking the Honda.

"Excuse me sir, just wait a moment please," he shouted. .

Danny froze; what the fuck was this all about, it just didn't make sense, no way would a uniform boy know him, neither would a uniform give him a tug for the blag, especially as firearms were used, it had to be something simple and a misunderstanding, it had to be.

As PC Evans walked towards Danny, his two way radio crackled into life: "All units, all mobiles, a serious armed robbery has taken place this morning in St Albans, be on the lookout for anything suspicious, do not under circumstances approach any suspects." Bloody hell, thought PC Evans, someone's going to see some action, all I've got is a bloody tax disc two days out of date.

Chapter 15

Gandamak, Northern Afghanistan

Night falls with the speed of an assassins' bullet in the Hindu Kush, there is no twilight- its light, and then it's dark. In the harsh winter months in Northern Afghanistan, the temperature drops to -20c in moments. The town of Gandamak had fallen silent before the inky blackness had descended.

In the alley way, which ran at right angles to the town square, and which housed the most wanted man in the world, two figures stood hunched in opposite doorways cradling burning cigarettes in an attempt to stave off the bitter night air; no one else moved.

In the inauspicious hovel that was situated a hundred meters to the north of the town square, Mike Tobin and his three comrades were wide eyed and buzzing, the adrenalin rushing, uncontrolled, through their bodies as they finalised the coming night's activities.

"One more time," said Mike as they rechecked the armoury that was spread out before them. All four men had checked their weaponry every day, at least six times since they had been holed up in the semi- derelict building that was a favoured habitat of the local peasants, and which caused little interest to the inhabitants of Gandamak.

All four men had the latest PVS-17s, a night vision goggle that enabled the user to operate in the darkest night as if they were in full daylight. There were Four M 84 flash bang grenades (wrapped in high density plastic to keep the noise down to a minimum, but maximise the effect), which happened to cause temporary blindness and massive disorientation, as the chemical reaction of magnesium and ammonia treated the recipients to a visit from a supa nova. There were four Arwen tear gas canisters; these were really back up, and for emergency use if the extraction met complications, as were the six Claymore anti-personnel mines, although Mike was planning on leaving these as a present on the outskirts of town just in case any of the locals wanted to play hero and give chase. Each trooper had the latest Sig Sauer P226 tactical pistol, manufactured to take a suppressor. This was the weapon of choice, and this was the weapon that was going to see action tonight, starting with the two condemned men in the alley who were about to light up their last cigarettes, of this lifetime anyway.

Finalising this array of warfare, there were four MAC-11 SMGs compacts, able to fire off an incredible 1600rpm; a favoured sub machine gun of the SAS to use at close quarters, and also capable of carrying a suppressor.

Mike opened the first aid kit and withdrew a small phial of colourless liquid- it was in fact a fast acting paralytic drug developed in the laboratories of a well known UK pharmaceutical company named Succinylchlorine. With rock steady hands, he broke open the small glass jar and inserted a syringe into the neck, carefully sucking the liquid into the plastic tube.

"Fucking Mother Theresa," came the comment from Jock Wallace, sitting immediately opposite Mike, and watching his every move.

"Once we get this inside the target, he's out for eight hours," retorted Mike. Changing the subject, he then asked: "So how's the wheels then, Jock?"

"All fuelled up and ready to go," replied Jock confidently. He had bought an Old Russian Volga from a trader in Kabul the previous week, it looked and was a shit heap, but no one in the regiment could touch Jock when it came to engines and this little baby was going to deliver them to the Rendezvous point, no problem. Whilst once again not drawing any curious looks from the locals.

"Right," said Mike. "We go in thirty minutes, so here's the brief..."

All three troopers stopped their cleaning and polishing, and looked attentively towards Mike. They had guessed it was a snatch, but were about to find out whom. It was always considered imperative on a black mission that team members were all treated on a strictly need to know basis, and when to know. As tough as these men were, no man alive could withstand modern day interrogation techniques for extended periods, so if any one was captured, or the mission compromised, during the long wait in the town they knew little to tell, which would actually make their interrogation far longer and considerably more painful than if they had known anything. They knew the risks.

Mike continued: " Inside that house that we've been watching these last four weeks is a target very valuable to our lords and masters," he said almost in a matter of fact way.

"Well there's a fucking surprise, "chortled Jock, "And I thought we were going to buy the place." The others laughed,

"Osama bin Laden," said Mike trying to be as measured as he could, but those three words were enough to wipe the grins off the faces of the assembled snatch squad. No one said a word for several seconds, then in total unison the tension was broken as the three SAS troopers said "Fucking hell, " and burst out laughing.

"So," Mike continued, knowing he had their full attention. "Let's keep it simple. Davey and Jim, you two walk down the alley and slot the two guards, remember they look like a couple of Afghan shepherds, but you can bet they're the bollocks, so no chances. Jock and me will drive the motor up and take out the front door, the same time as you lob the flash bangs through the window, we are pretty sure there are four hostiles in the house plus the target, so remember all the training back in the killing house at Hereford and we'll be fine. I will take the target, get him knocked out, and Jock will help me get him into the boot of the motor. The four hostiles are down to Davey and Jim. I want to be out and on the road in forty-five seconds." The other three nodded confirming, they could achieve this.

"Once on the road," continued Mike, "we head due south. I'm going to cross into Pakistan using the border crossing at Torkham."

"Why not go straight through the Khyber Pass?" asked Davey. "It's quicker and there's more traffic to get lost amongst."

Mike acknowledged a fair point. "Davey, if the shit hits the fan and we get into a fire fight on the border, then the chances of us getting through are greater at Torkham where the border guards are less well trained and would not be expecting us to go that way. We just don't know how quick the word will get out that we've got Allah's first premier lieutenant in the boot."

They all laughed at the preposterousness of the situation. Without waiting for the group to comment on the merits of the extra time in the mountains of Afghanistan by crossing at Torkham, Mike continued: " Once inside Pakistan, we head north to Peshawar, about one hundred klicks south there's a flat piece of land, a small valley where we RV with a Little Bird. There's just enough ground for him to land."

The Little Bird was an all weather light attack aircraft with a fuel range of four hundred and thirty klicks, and was capable of carrying the five people who would be waiting. "The Bird takes us into Islamabad Airfield where there is currently a joint training exercise occurring between the Pakistan Air Force and the Royal Air Force"

"Mighty convenient," grinned Davey.

Mike continued: "Once we hit Islamabad we all transfer to a Hercules already scheduled to fly out to Brize Norton, and that, chaps, is our work complete, piece of piss, any questions?"

"Yeah," said Jock, "Seeing how high profile this is, how come the Yanks aren't involved? They want him more than us, and it's not their way to trust us."

"Because," Mike grinned," they haven't been told about the party."

The others shook their heads in disbelief. "Any other little gems you want to tell us about?" asked Jim.

"No, that's it, shall we go?" enquired Mike.

In fact, Mike had one more piece of the jigsaw that he felt no need to disclose. He was going to have to let the British security services contact over in Islamabad know they were on their way. Although this had all been pre arranged, the exact date of the extraction could not be pre arranged due to the unpredictable weather, so Mike needed to fire off an encrypted message as soon as they collected the package. This, ironically, would go via GCHQ, from the satellite phone which would take a nano second to deliver. However, the danger was that it was going to alert any listeners just as the original message had done so several weeks earlier. This time though, the listeners back at GCHQ were ready and waiting, and had been for several days now. They were primed to inform Islamabad immediately. By the time any hostiles had picked up the message and passed it upwards realising there was mischief afoot, Mike and the boys would be long gone, and well, that was the assumption anyway.

The timing of the snatch was of paramount importance to its success; like all military operations preparation and rehearsal was the key. What happened on the battlefield was determined by the planning, and Mike and the squad had this down to a fine art. Davey and Jim McClougin, who was known as Badger (due to a period in his life several years previously, when he had lived in a badgers sett for nine consecutive nights, somewhere in Kent, whilst training with the boys from Special Branch) left the hovel that had been home for the last few weeks by the front opening, took one side of the road each and made their way towards the square. The walk was to take three minutes forty-five seconds as they traversed the square, keeping as close to the ramshackle buildings as possible to avoid any late night curiosity. Mike and Jock slid out of the back entrance and into the car for the one minute fifty five second drive that would see them at the front of the house to coincide with the arrival of the other two.

It was four minutes past 2am as Davey and the Badger turned into the alley; even the hour had been debated thoroughly, and all agreed on the tried and tested practice that any surprise assault should occur when the enemy are at their most vulnerable, both physically and mentally, and this was the early morning hours between two and four am.

Both guards were extinguishing their cigarettes when they simultaneously spotted the two shadowy figures approaching. The weeks of inactivity had made them careless, and neither heard the double discharge from two silenced Sig Saurs pistols as two cartridges entered each man's body, one each through the skull just above the right ear, and one each through the chest cavity, turning their two main vital organs into a scrambled mush before they hit the floor. Hopefully

Allah and the virgins were ready for them.

As the Volga, lights now off, turned into the alley Davey and the Badger were by the door of the house securing the plastic explosives to the door frame, so far so good. This next move was due to take less than two minutes: to get in, silence the guards, suppress Bin Laden and bundle him into the boot of the Volga. Mike jumped out of the passengers' door, thirty feet from the house. Ten seconds later, as he lobbed the first Flash Bang through the window, Davey detonated the plastics which hurled the door inward as it splintered into a thousand deadly shards. Jim the Badger followed the shattered door into the blinding light the Flash Bang had created; with his Night Goggles he saw four burly men, two to his right, two to his left, and all had looks of fear and astonishment on their faces, but all four had AK 47 sub machine guns to hand. Jim knew he could not take down all four, as they were already gathering their senses and reaching for their weapons. All those hours of training back at Sterling Lines came to fruition- Jim didn't consider the men to his left, he fired off four rounds, two each into the two men on his right, dropping them like stones. Before they hit the bare floor, the other two to his right suffered the same ending as Davey, who had followed Jim into the building, and despatched his victims with the same confidence that his comrade had exhibited.

As Davey and Jim crouched to observe any other guards, Mike had gone between them and in a single action kicked the internal door, which led to the only other room in the building, off its hinges and despatched another Flash Bang into the middle of the room. Mike followed the grenade into the windowless room and immediately spotted over in the far corner the shape of a man huddled up and trying to cover himself with one of the rough blankets that were strewn on the bed- and which up to a minute ago Osama Bin Laden, his quarry, had been sleeping soundly on. Mike was the only member of the team carrying the MAC SMG; as last into the building, he would either need a fast repeating weapon if things did not work out, or nothing and nothing was the case.

Mike crossed the room with lightning speed, ripped the blanket off the last live terrorist in the house, and brought the butt of the MAC down onto the temple of the man who cowered in front of him, Osama Bin Laden. For a fleeting second, Mike's training to never dwell on the battlefield left him; here right in front of him was a crumpled man, helpless- was it really the same person who had wreaked carnage on the United States of America and had half the armed forces of the Western World hunting him? To Bin Laden it must have felt like the Four Horsemen Of The Apocalypse had come calling, and Mike could only stare in near disbelief that the man lying in front of him, bruised and broken, was World public enemy number one. All this happened in under a second, and Mike was now back in charge of himself and the troop.

"All clear here and ready to move out." he called.

"And here," replied The Badger.

"And here," replied Davey.

Whilst Jim and Davey started a meticulous search of the building, collecting each and every scrap of paper no matter how obscure, then stuffing it all into their Bergens for the spooks to pour over, Mike had opened up the first aid kit, removed the loaded syringe, and with a quick flick of the cylinder to remove any accumulated air bubbles, (well after all this work he didn't really want to send a rogue air bubble to Bin Laden's heart and kill him now), firmly jabbed the needle into the terrorist's neck and pushed the plunger with little finesse, down as far as it would go.

As he removed the needle from Bin Laden's neck, Jock hurried into the room. Without saying a word, Jock grabbed Bin Laden's feet, Mike grabbed his shoulders, and together they carried him out to the alley where the Volga was ticking over. The boot was open, and they unceremoniously dumped him into the waiting chamber and banged it shut. As they climbed into their seats, Davey and Jim came out of the house, now a morgue, and jumped into their seats in the rear of the vehicle. The decision had been made not to torch the house, it would only raise the locals quicker and furthermore, once the shit hit the fan, Bin Laden's mob were hardly likely to send round the local SOCO, or Scenes of Crimes Officers.

The whole operation was exactly within the time frame planned, and the Volga slid gently out of town without a soul noticing; well they sure as hell must have heard the door implode if nothing else, still, in this part of the world people tend not to see any thing extraordinary, and Mike and the troop hoped this would be the case and buy them enough time to get to the border.

As the Volga left town and hit the unlit semi-metalled road, Mike told Jock to slow right down. Mike jumped out of the car and walked thirty meters behind, placing the Claymores at regular intervals. If there were any hostiles left in the village, this would stop them in a hurry, and if there weren't, then some unlucky bastard would meet an untimely end sometime in the morning; still, life was cheap round these parts, and Bin Laden for a couple of locals was a good enough swap.

As Mike placed the last mine, he removed the Sat phone from his pack and sent the coded message up into space that would get the Little Bird airborne, and them out of this Godforsaken land. With a quick glance upwards, as if to wish the message luck, he caught up with the motor and regained his seat. The journey down to the border was uneventful, if that was possible considering the prize safely ensconced in the trunk.

As the Volga approached the border, it was noticeable that the increase in human flotsam and jetsam seemed to be endlessly meandering both towards the border and away from it. The dramatically painted Lorries that the Pakistani truck drivers loved to adorn with pictures of their loved ones, their homes and any other significance in their lives, had now ground to a halt, but the cars and pedestrians were still moving, and the checkpoint was now in view. No words were spoken between the four SAS men, but each had placed their MAC SMG within close proximity and placed them on continuous fire; any trouble and they would have to shoot their way across the border, probably leaving the prisoner behind and heading into the mountains. The crossing point was now upon them, and as they drew up Mike wound down his window to do the talking; he was fluent in Urdu and hoped he would be the only one needing to talk. The Volga drew level with a heavily moustached and heavily armed official, who peered into the motor, looked Mike in the eye, and waved them through, no checking of papers, passports or contents, nothing Jack Shit.

As the motor swung north, heading towards the RV point, Jock spoke first.

"Fucking hell," he exclaimed as he let out a whistle that is a universal exclamation for a lucky escape. The tension in the motor evaporated as the troopers, who had been ready for any scenario, relaxed knowing they were nearly home and dry.

Mike stared straight ahead. The intuition, sixth sense, déjà vu that had kept him alive for all these years had kicked into overdrive- that crossing was wrong, it was too easy, and it was like they were expecting them.

That seemed impossible, even if somehow word had got out they would have been gunned down and not allowed to cross. Could it be paranoia as this was to be Mike's last mission? Nonetheless, Mike had a feeling of deep unease.

And well he should.

Chapter 16

The Tora Bora mountains

Throughout the centuries, the arrogance of the British Army in underestimating its opposition had caused the Empire to lose more conflicts than it should. The current enemies of the civilised world were hidden in the near impregnable caves of the Tora Bora mountain range- to be more precise two thousand Al Qaeda soldiers of freedom were living in the inside of one of the many peaks in the neighbourhood of the village of Tora Bora. Soaring to a majestic thirteen thousand feet, the mountain of Gree Khil, which housed these pirates, looked down almost mockingly at the village,

The great irony was that in the 1980s, these mountains had been developed into sophisticated bunkers to house Afghan warlords and regular militia men by the best engineers America had to offer. The Russian invasion of Afghanistan had not suited the Americans, and so they had blasted great chambers up to a thousand feet deep into the caves of Tora Bora, to assist the Afghans against the common foe. Whether this assisted the Afghans in humiliating the superior Russian forces remains debatable, but what is known is that the labyrinth of tunnels was being put to good use by the now enemies of the USA.

In the mountain of Gree Khil, there were six levels that contained every conceivable commodity with which an army could survive. The hydroelectric power was sourced by mountain streams, and six inch steel doors were positioned throughout the complex in the event of a gas attack or worse.

On the third level stood rows of computer banks,; this entire level looked like the NASA control room at

Houston, in fact it had been NASA engineers that had designed and installed the equipment that was now the centre of attention and causing much excitement.

Osama Bin Laden stood in the centre of the hall, head bowed in deep conversation with one of his cohorts.

"The British are so stupid," he was saying, "They have taken the bait in their excitement to capture me, phase one of the plan is complete, they have now crossed into Pakistan. In another hour they intend to rendezvous with their aircraft, our allies are waiting and Osama Bin Laden will be killed in the ambush, and the great Satan will have his revenge and go back to sleep." Both men laughed conspiratorially.

Indeed the plan, as daring as it was, had worked. A full second before Mike's radio communication had arrived at GCHQ, it had been picked up by the equipment on level three of the high peak known as Gree Khil.

The engineers of Al Qaeda had been expecting the communiqué, just as the listeners at GCHQ had. From the very first radio message picked up by the drone all those months ago, the entire discovery of Bin Laden had been a charade, masterminded by Mr Bin Laden himself. If the western agencies were to believe he was dead, he could once again travel the world with the impunity he had had before the events of 9/11.

Now the final phase to the plan was about to unfold. It was just as outrageous as the first part; the false Bin Laden would have to be destroyed inside Pakistan, but the papers that had been collected from the house in Gandamak, which bore genuine handwriting from Bin Laden, would have to find their way to the security services of Britain and America to substantiate that the body left in Pakistan was indeed that of Osama Bin Laden. Could the great power of the West be fooled by such a hoax? Bin Laden and his generals knew the answer to that.

It was unthinkable to the British that their defence systems could be compromised, but that was indeed the case, and nowhere less than GCHQ where three senior civil servants, who each had access to top priority state secrets, were all Al Qaeda fundamentalists. All three were sleepers, introduced into the British way of life in their early teens, and left to adapt to and infiltrate the establishment wherever they could. There was no contact from their masters year after year, but all knew that the call would come, and when it did they must be ready. And so it was that on a cold December night in late 2001, Sally Dixon had returned to her one bedroom flat in the centre of Cheltenham and made the call, which would end the lives of people she would never know.

Osama Bin Laden, who had just been notified of Sally Dixon's message and was holding court with his trusted few, commented: "How can we trust these treacherous pirates?"

"Because, Sire," came the reply "They answer to one God and that is the US Dollar. When we get confirmation from our source in Britain that you are dead, they get 200,000 dollars, and not before."

"Very good," replied Bin Laden "The next few hours are critical then"

"Indeed" was the answer.

Chapter 17

The North West Frontier

The border was now well behind Mike and the boys. No one spoke as they journeyed north, steadily making their way nearer the RV. The terrain was unforgiving, but the Volga never missed a beat. Mike was still troubled with the ease of the crossing, but he kept his thoughts to himself. If there was any thing tangible he would have voiced his concerns, but as the Leader he couldn't show he was spooked by a hunch, no, he would remain extra diligent until they were out of these mountains.

Jock tapped Mike on the shoulder and pointed ahead. Both men could see the faint outline of the terrain as it levelled out, this was the RV point. Mike checked his watch, five minutes before the Little Bird landed. The plan was for the Volga to station itself at the end of the valley, flash the lights a couple of times and rely on the skills of the pilot to land the plane as near to them as possible. There was to be no Hollywood style lighting up of the air strip, the natives in these parts were mighty suspicious and mighty dangerous.

The land was now flat enough for Mike to cut the lights on the motor and cautiously make his way round to the head of the valley. All the troopers were now on full alert, this was the last place things could go seriously tits up.

The Volga was in position and waiting when four things happened almost simultaneously. The faint hum of the Little Bird's engine came into earshot, the night sky lit up with six ark lights all trained on the Volga, the air was filled with a loudhailer which instructed the car's occupants to leave the car immediately (although the command was in the local dialect of Pashto all of the troop understood the order), and surrounding the car were four UAZ 469s Russian all terrain jeeps, each full to the brim with local tribesmen. The four SAS soldiers were blinded by the light; the positioning of the jeeps had sealed off any escape route in the car, and their only chance was to exit the car and attempt a fire fight, but things didn't look good.

As they began slowly to leave the car, each man trying to distance himself from the others to increase the target they made and buy some time, a streak of yellow light filled the night sky as it soared air bound from behind a small hillock half way down the runway. It was another Russian leftover, a MANPADS, which was a Man-Portable Air Defence System, fired from the shoulder of a man. This was the FIM-43c model, otherwise known generally as a SAM or Surface to Air Missile. This model, when launched, would lock onto the thermal signature of its target and be drawn in by the heat of the engine.

Mesmerised by the trajectory of the missile, all the troopers could do was watch in horrific fascination as it traversed the night sky before, after ten seconds, it found and detonated inside the engine of the Little Bird. The plane disintegrated in a fireball. It was like the movies. The crew had no chance for evasive manoeuvring, they were just too near the landing point, it was probably for the best- if they had been three klicks out they would have still had no chance, just longer to acclimatise to their death.

As the remnants of the plane fell to the ground, another rocket was launched, and this time it came from the back of one of the UAZs, maybe fifty meters away. This was a GTGM or Ground to Ground missile; another destructive weapon that could be launched from a man's shoulder, this was a RPG-7 or rocket propelled grenade, and in under a second it had torn into the Volga, causing another spectacular explosion. With Bin Laden still secreted in the trunk when the missile hit, it was highly unlikely there would be any remains left, let alone any identifiable body parts.

It was for situations like this that the SAS trained its troops so vigorously; no matter what the odds, in any given confrontation there was always a point where an opportunity came in which the overwhelmed might just grab the proverbial lifeline, and so it was that as the Volga exploded the attention of the aggressors was wavering between the two fireballs and the troopers who were just clear of the car. It had been no coincidence how the four men had exited the vehicle. Badger and Davey went to the left hand side, both men ten feet apart, and Mike and Jock in the same position went to the right of the car. All four men instinctively knew this was the chance to resist their imminent execution. As one, they raised the concealed MAC SMGs that were fully primed, and blasted at the headlights of the UAZs. All hell let loose, with the lamps on the jeeps being extinguished, and several screams from the bandits who would have been mortally injured in the frenzy. Mike and Jock broke for cover to their right, and Jim and Davey to their left. Although there were several tribesmen down, there was no way of knowing how many were out there, and now the troop was divided there was little chance of regrouping. Mike and Jock holed up behind a jagged rock, still only twenty meters from the killing zone.

"Fucking hell" Mike said, trying to catch his breath and assess the damage, "That's Bin Laden gone, did you see if the others made ground?" he enquired of Jock.

"Nope" replied Jock, his eyes darting around the

surrounding area constantly, " It was too bright and too quick, how the hell did that happen, where did those fuckers come from?" he asked.

"Fuck knows," replied Mike, "and at this time I don't give a shit, but they were waiting and this was an eyes only operation, so someone's got a big problem back home, but we've got a bigger problem right here so let's stay focused on getting out of these mountains alive" he said.

"What about the other two?" asked Jock.

"You know the procedure," Mike said. "We're in a hostile land, separated from them with no means of contact, we still have evidence from the house back in Gandamak that we need to get delivered, so if we see them, fine, but our immediate priority is to get somewhere safer. We don't know how many hostiles are still out there or what fire power they're holding, so we're going to crawl out of here the way we came until we can circle around this area and head north on foot."

Jock wanted to remonstrate with Mike, but he knew Mike was right; it was every man for himself in a situation as fraught as this. Jesus, it was hardly going to be a walk in the park getting out of these badlands as it was.

As Mike and Jock began the painfully slow crawl to engineer some distance between themselves and the bad guys, Mike had that uneasy feeling return, but this time with good justification. He motioned to Jock with a closed fist, which was a battlefield gesture to stop.

"Jock" he said "Where the fuck are the bad guys? They had us bang to rights, even if we made our ground they could have flattened the entire area with the ordinance they've got."

"I was wondering that myself, Boss" Jock whispered. "But right now I don't give a toss. If we get out of here I'll kiss Allah's arse and answer that question then."

"Fair enough" came the reply.

As the sun rose to the east, Mike and Jock continued to slither between the rocks and grassy knolls, trying to distance themselves from the devastating scene of a few hours earlier; they had covered no more than fifty meters in the three hours since the ambush.

Standing high above them was the leader of the tribesmen and forty followers. The leader had been observing their progress through his night vision goggles initially, and as dawn had broken, he had reverted to normal vision. His eyes were trained to spot a small animal at fifty meters in this hostile environment, so observing Mike and Jock was no problem.

"Just as we were instructed," he said to the man to his immediate left. "Two to escape and two to die."

"Allah has looked favourably on us this night" came the reply.

"Tell the men they will get their Yankee dollars, and then take the jeep back to the border and inform our friends all has gone to plan" instructed the commander, and with that he turned to the rear of ledge he and his men had occupied since the fire fight. Lying semi-conscious, bleeding, bruised and battered, were two members of Britain's elite Special Forces, the SAS.

With a malevolent smirk the leader of the guerrillas addressed them in his native tongue: "Two of you go and two of you stay, and you my friends stay, whoever your God is, give him my regards," and with that he withdrew his pistol and at point blank range discharged a single round into the forehead of each man. Davey and the Badger died, thankfully instantaneously.

Chapter 18

Century House, 4 weeks later

You would think that the clandestine operations involved in the security of the United Kingdom would be housed away from the public at large, and hidden in a remote Scottish Glen or some where else of that ilk, but nothing could be farther from the truth. The Secret Intelligence Service, otherwise known as M15, or The Firm, occupied the building at 85 Albert Embankment, Vauxhall Cross, London. Just to make sure it was unmissable it was nicknamed Lego Land by those in the know, and to take one look at the building is to understand why. In recent years the building has featured in no less than three James Bond films, and on September 20th 2000 the eight floor was severely damaged by a Russian RPG-22 anti-tank missile launched somewhere behind Westminster Bridge Road. The Real IRA was held accountable.

It was rumoured that when the building had been constructed, a tunnel under the Thames linking Lego Land with Whitehall was incorporated to allow the comings and goings of senior politicians in times of state emergencies.

It was on this late February morning that the Prime Minister Tony Blair had availed himself of the rumoured tunnel, and walked under the river and into the cellars of Century House, where he was met by two ex marines who courteously escorted him to the 9th floor.

The current Chief of Operations, Sir Richard Dearlove, was sitting at the head of a large rosewood table, with four colleagues, two either side.

"Good Morning, Prime Minister" he said

measurably.

"Morning, Richard" replied the PM with his normal and public chirpiness, "I must say, since I got the news, little else has been on my mind."

I bet there hasn't, thought Sir Richard, if *you can take the credit for the end of the greatest terrorist threat to the West in the history of mankind you'll probably get a statue in Admiralty Gate*, but these thoughts he kept to himself, instead he offered introductions of the four people around the table: "To my right is Dr David Davies. David heads up the team at the Home Office Pathology and Forensic laboratories at Porton Down, it's David who has been assessing the artefacts that came out of the house in Gandamak." The two men shook hands, the PM still beaming, hoping to put the assembled party at ease. Sir Richard continued: "Next to David is Major Sebastian Morley, who heads up the team down in Hereford. I believe you already know each other." The PM gave Major Morley a conspiratorial wink, which was a little unsettling for the Major considering the subject matter.

"Next" Sir Richard continued, "is John Smith, Head of Counter Intelligence, and based down at the establishment in Hampshire. John and his team have been chatting with the two troopers that made it out of Pakistan, and brought home the bacon that David has been cooking." For the first time that morning the PM shook the hand of John Smith, but without his normal familiarity, he knew what John Smith did, he certainly didn't approve, but he was also pragmatic enough to understand that when it came to the defence of the realm there were occasions that warranted the use of such people and their methods. In bygone times John Smith would have been known as the Witchfinder General, extracting confessions from poor souls before burning them at the stake. He would have been interrogating the troopers mercilessly since they arrived back to the safety of Blighty.

"And last. But by no means least," continued Sir Richard, "Sally Dixon. Sally has been seconded from GCHQ to help with translations that may be needed, Sally is one of our Bright Young Stars, and co-incidentally, Prime Minister, she was actually the one who was first to pick up the original transmission from Afghanistan." The PM had his beaming face back on, he was comfortable with Bright Young Things, especially women.

"I'm delighted to meet you Sally" he said congenially.

The Prime Minister took a chair at the far end of the table, everyone else followed suit and Sir Richard started procedures. "Right Prime Minister, we will start at the beginning, everyone in this room knows their own piece in this matter, so it will be advantageous that we all have a clear picture of events as they unfolded."

"Agreed" said the PM

Agreed thought Sally, but just sat waiting her turn, expressionless.

"Right then" said Sir Richard, "Major Morley, if you would be so kind."

"You are all aware of the circumstances that bring us together today," the Major began. "As you know, we inserted a specialised team into Afghanistan, following the information our friends at GCHQ collated." He smiled at Sally and continued, "It had to be a black operation on a strictly need to know basis, the potential rewards were the likely collapse of Al-Qaeda as a potential threat to the West for many years to come. I used four of my top tactical mountain cadre, and the mission was led by the most experienced man we have at Hereford, no one in the history of the service has extracted more hostages and prisoners from behind enemy lines than Mike Tobin." No one spoke; they were all waiting for the Major's take on what went wrong,

He continued: "The mission was so secret there were no means of tracking the troop, once they were inserted into Afghanistan they were on their own, and if they had been captured we would have denied their existence, at worst we would have claimed they had gone rogue and turned Bounty Hunters for the twenty five million dollar reward on Bin Laden's head. There was a prearranged signal that was to be fired off if the mission was successful, this duly occurred five weeks after the insertion, it meant they had the quarry and were inside Pakistan within two hours of a RV point."

"Go on," said the PM, frowning.

"So our first communication with the troop comes after nothing for over a month, we launch a plane to collect them from a small plateau inside Pakistan but deep in the Mountains, even the Pilot is not given the co-ordinates until he's airborne, then what happens is nothing, absolutely nothing. We've got a Hercules ticking over on the tarmac at Islamabad, air traffic control ready to land the rescue plane right up to the Hercules, a virtual shutdown of the entire airport until we get them in and out, but nothing shows."

Major Morley took a long drink of water, then continued: "Of course we can't ask the Cousins(a colloquial name for American military and secret service) if they've picked any thing up, they're still happily systematically rearranging the landscape of the Tora Bora Mountains, blissfully unaware what we're up to. So after the deadline has passed, we have to assume the plane has either crash landed in the pick up zone or flown into the side of a mountain, either before or after the pick up. At this point our friends at Cheltenham are able to divert a satellite over the area,

114

plus we get an AWAC airborne, but that's as much as we can do without alerting the Cousins we've got some sort of operation going down in the area. Anyhow the AWAC has picked up the wreckage of the plane, and I mean wreckage, it didn't take long to realise that the recovery plane had suffered a direct hit from a SAM, we then had the AWAC produce a satellite photograph of the entire area within a five kilometre radius, and we picked up the burnt out shell of a car, plus several bodies, no doubt about what happened the boys were ambushed, and I don't mean they were unlucky and stumbled on a local posse of bad guys, I mean these people were waiting for them."

"What happened next? asked the PM.

"As far as we are concerned, that's the end of it," said Major Morley. "We've posted our people Missing in Action and informed the relatives they were lost on a training exercise in Norway. Then after three weeks, right out of the blue, we get a call from British Consulate in Islamabad who informs us two very emaciated vagrants were seeking asylum but refusing to answer any questions until they had spoken to me directly, any where else in the world they would have been chucked out on their ears, but this being Pakistan the consulate thought he had better check with me, and from there it didn't take long to establish it was indeed Mike Tobin and Jock Wallace. They had walked through the Mountains and into Islamabad, it took them over three weeks and, quite honestly, it was one of the most incredible feats of endurance I've come across in all my years in the SAS."

"So much so," said Sir Richard, "that we were not comfortable with their story, to walk out of that hostile environment is in itself damn near impossible, but presumably they were also being hunted by the insurgents that ambushed them and needed to take extra precautions. Furthermore, how did they even walk away from an ambush in an alien environment, one which the attackers lived and breathed in? Surely if the bandits were able to take out a plane, they could have eliminated the squad with considerable ease, it just didn't fit whichever way we looked at it. They did carry out several documents and maps from the house in Gandamak which David will talk about shortly, but apart from that we were deeply suspicious that somewhere down the piece they had sold out."

"So what did you do?" enquired the PM.

"We kept them out of sight, separated them, got them on the next flight to Brize Norton, and then sent them down to our Training establishment in Hampshire where John, here de-briefed them."

The Prime Minister was not looking forward to what John Smith had to say, and hoped he would be spared the details of the "de-brief."

As a highly trained counter espionage officer, John Smith was trained to read people's minds by their body language and general demeanour, and it was right to show some deference towards the Prime Minister of Great Britain.

"The two soldiers in question," he began, "Mike Tobin and Jock Wallace, are two highly skilled Special Forces operators; both of them have been on several black missions previously and have always proved their loyalty and commitment beyond reproach. If they have been turned or just gone native it was always going to be exceptionally difficult to get either one to confess, they have both been through all the interrogation techniques, and how to avoid talking, many times in their history with the Unit. However, as much as we train these soldiers to resist the modern art of interrogation, we are aware that there are occasions when the toughest of men will turn renegade, and so we have certain methods, developed and refined over many years, which even our most trusted personnel, be they soldiers or field operators from the security service, do not know how to resist. There is no need for me to explain what we do, only to inform you of the result. The soldier in charge on the ground, Mike Tobin, is a highly skilled operative, he told us of easy passage through the border on the way out, he said it had been nagging him right through the long walk out of Pakistan, he even told us he couldn't understand how they had managed to evade capture, at the very least, at the ambush. At a certain point in the interview we informed him of the death of his two colleagues, his reaction showed us he suspected they had not made it and that was right, so all in all, gentlemen and lady, we have concluded that Mike Tobin and Jock Wallace have told us the entire truth as they see it, and I would like to say they are two lucky people to be alive today but I can't."

"What do you mean?" enquired the PM.

"Well, Sir," continued John Smith "There is nothing conclusive to suggest otherwise but like Tobin, myself and members of my team spend our entire waking hours questioning peoples motives, their actions and their logic. We are continuously looking for the slightest flaw in our subjects that may denote a potential lie or even a half truth, we are suspicious by nature, and by training we have to read hidden meanings into everything we investigate, and if by distrusting everyone we save one life we have done our job. It is without foundation, but nevertheless my belief, that somehow this whole Bin Laden situation has been a set up and we walked right in. In a nutshell I suspect we have a leak"

There was silence in the room, for several seconds; Sally Dixon went as pale as death, she nearly gagged and if she had been asked to talk next would not have been able to. She looked at John Smith and the thought of having a little chat with him down on the Farm in Hampshire nearly caused her to pass out there and then.

"So," Sir Richard said after several long silent moments "Let's hear what David has to tell us."

David Evans was a typical boffin- bespectacled, overweight and with a generally scruffy appearance, sweating profusely in the presence of the number one citizen of the country, but always comfortable on his subject matter. He began:

"I have examined all the items the soldiers brought out of Afghanistan, and we have traced the paper certain articles were written on, we have traced the DNA that was abundant, and we have taken finger prints. We have translated the writings through Sally, we have tracked the dust particles that were present and we have traced the source of the ink that was used in the writings of the documents that were brought back. We have analysed the evidence more extensively than anything we have ever done before, and I can say without a shadow of a doubt the person in that room was Osama Bin Laden"

Sir Richard and John Smith exchanged glances, and it was Sir Richard, head of the British Secret Service, who spoke.

David," he said very slowly "The man in the house in Gandamak was surrounded by all the evidence you have confirmed as belonging to Bin Laden, and no doubt it does, but what evidence do you have that the paperwork that was in the same room was in any way processed by this man, or putting it another way, what direct evidence have you obtained from the man we originally believed to be Bin Laden?"

David Davies starred into the piecing blue eyes of Sir Richard Dearlove for a very long time, at some point he realised all eyes were on him and he needed to reply to the Boss.

"None, Sir" was his answer.

"Thank you David" said Sir Richard "Now have you anything to add Sally?" he enquired.

Sally Dixon's day was disintegrating whilst she stood by watching British Intelligence begin to unravel the plot she had been complicit with. She had regained her composure from the initial shock of hearing there was suspicion that it was a hoax. Before the meeting started she was clear in her mind that her job would be to confirm that all the manuscripts found were of course the work of Bin Laden; as a student of Language she knew all written work carried its author's signature just as significantly as all the finger prints and the DNA David Davies had found. However she quickly needed to change tack.

"It is my opinion, Sir, that the translations that I was asked to do on the various pieces of work I was given bore a startling resemblance to that of previous works by Mr Bin Laden, and I would say they were almost definitely written by him," she stated, and very pleased with herself too, she felt a lot better. What she or any one else in the room failed to spot was the lightning quick glance Sir Richard and John Smith exchanged as Sally finished speaking.

Before Sally could continue, Tony Blair interjected. "So if I'm hearing and understanding this correctly, you are saying the man we snatched in Gandamak was not Bin Laden?" he enquired of the assembled experts.

Sir Richard spoke "What we are saying, PM, is the evidence we have is substantial but not conclusive, it is our job to prove beyond a shadow of doubt that the man who unfortunately died that night in the mountains of Pakistan was Osama Bin Laden. There is, although highly unlikely, the possibility this was an elaborate hoax; until we are sure beyond any reasonable doubt, we cannot assume otherwise."

The PM looked stunned. "Do you mean to tell me," he asked, " that there is the possibility that if this was a hoax the people who were in the house knew there was going to be an armed force which would undoubtedly kill them, no, have to kill them?"

"Prime Minister," began Sir Richard, "these people are zealots, to them death is something to be rejoiced in, to die for one's religion is to invite martyrdom, and they are no different than the suicide bombers who plague the streets of all Islamic countries."

"My God," said the PM. "So if this was some elaborate plot too convince us Bin Laden is dead, what in heavens name do I tell POTUS?"

"Well, PM," said Sir Richard, "I believe at this moment in time the Cousins are blissfully unaware of our attempt to liberate Mr Bin Laden and therefore we really have nothing to tell them. Let sleeping dogs lie is the phrase I think"

"Yes of course." the PM replied "But where exactly do we go from here?"

This time it was the turn of John Smith to reply.

"Prime Minister, our priorities remain the same, we have to establish the authenticity of the principal, but now we shall approach it from a different perspective."

"Go on" the PM said.

"If we now assume the whole incident was a charade from start to finish, there is, without the shadow of doubt, a traitor within our establishment. As clever as this little escapade has been, it could not have happened without some inside help from here in the UK."

Sir Richard nodded in agreement, and instructed his head of intelligence to continue.

"And here's where we get a break," continued John,

"because the operation was code blue, here at Century House there are, outside of the five of us in this room, six people who were in the loop on this operation. Assuming we five are all innocent, then we have six people to investigate."

"How long do you expect it will take? asked the PM.

"Prime Minister, we have to build a picture of these six people's lives for the last four months, and that means scrutinising every element of their work and private lives, from phone calls to where they go, where they've been, what they've bought, every miniscule aspect of their existence, and when we've done all that we would hope to have one, but not more than two, suspects, who we will then have to investigate further back, and then, and only then, if we have one direct suspect, we would detain them under The Officials Secrets Act which would allow us to then formally interview them."

"And if all your people are in the clear, or have been too clever to make any detectable mistakes?" the PM asked.

"If that was the case, then Sir, I could confidently assure you that the man at Gandamak was indeed Osama Bin Laden, nobody can evade detection with the scrutiny that we will deploy" replied John Smith.

"How long before you can give me an answer?" the PM asked.

"From start to finish, employing all my personnel, four weeks, unless of course someone breaks early on, so in the meantime I would suggest we all return to our normal routines and wait for me and my team to report back" John answered.

"Prime Minister, I know this is not what you wanted to hear, however there is little collateral damage, the Cousins are none the wiser, apart from the tragic loss of two of our own, no harm will come out of this, no matter what the outcome." Sir Richard stated.

"Very well then," replied the PM. "thank you all for your hard work and dedication, we will reconvene when we are certain one way or the other."

Tony Blair rose from his chair, shook everyone's hand, and strode off to find his bodyguards before the walk back to Westminster. The meeting was over, and there was nothing else to be said or that could be done.

Sally Dixon was the first to leave; she exited the building alongside Westminster Bridge Road and decided to walk the fifteen minutes to her temporary accommodation just off the Elephant and Castle. The last two hours had been the worst of her life; the fantasy land she had inhabited for the last several years had imploded, from being a heroine of Allah's cause, a latter day Joan of Arc, the reality of being a traitor to her own country and the possibility of exposure and a life in Broadmoor was staring her in the face. She needed to think. She was to meet her handler in Borough Market the next morning at 11am to give a briefing on the meeting and the outcome, that in itself would be difficult, but she knew she couldn't run, so she would carry out the rendezvous and then perhaps take a well earned break, go to South America. However, Sir Richard had said there was no suspicion on anyone in the room todaythat thought lightened her gloom.

What Sally didn't see as she left Century House, were the two men on opposite sides of the road, who had been waiting for her departure all morning. As she headed down St Georges Road the two employees of the British Secret Service kept a respectful distance, but not for one moment did either of them let Sally out of sight.Sally with great relief reached her flat shut and bolted the front door, then in a moments madness which comes to us all in times of panic she removed her mobile from her bag and called her handler.

For many a long year the British Army were guilty of underestimating their opponents, this however was not the case with the British Security Services.

Chapter 19

The M3 motorway, the next day

The BMW 700 series with blacked out windows cruised past Fleet services, on the M3 heading south towards Hampshire. No one was interested; in this part of the world BMWs were no big deal, not when you had all the flash cars of the decadent footballers regularly flying up to their training grounds before returning home to their stately piles. People would surely have been interested though. if they knew where the car was heading, and who the occupants were, and the reason why the windows were blacked out.

In the rear of the car Sally Dixon was in pieces; two men had arrived on her doorstep early that morning, showed her their credentials, which she had instantly recognised as Security Services, and informed her their boss John Smith would like a chat- destination the Farm, Hampshire.

Chapter 20

SAS HQ Hereford

Mike Tobin had returned to Hereford following his two week enforced R&R. Since returning from Pakistan he had plenty of free time to contemplate his future. Whilst he had always planned to chuck it in after this mission, there had always been that nagging doubt in the back of his mind; would he miss the regiment and all the excitement that went with it? Well as far he was concerned, the botched mission had sealed his future. He had lost two comrades for no good reason and the writing was on the wall, it was time to go.

Major Sebastian Morley sat in the same chair in his office that he had when he'd briefed Mike on the mission all those weeks ago.

"Come in" he said, as Mike firmly knocked the door.

"Nice fortnight off, Mike?" he enquired.

"Usual stuff," answered Mike, "Got pissed, then got pissed some more. Anyhow, Sir, I'll get straight to the point, I'm calling it a day, so if you could get the paperwork sorted I think its best I go now."

Major Morley was not surprised. "Mike, is this due to the fuck up over in the badlands?"

"No sir," came the reply. "I was pretty sure this was going to be it whatever the outcome and it just cemented my thoughts when I heard the news."

"What you don't know, Mike," replied the Major, "is that the woman from GCHQ was the mole, and our friends at MI5 ousted her shortly after you and Jock got back, too late as far as you were concerned, but at least she's out of harms way now."

"What happened to her?" Mike enquired.

"As always in cases of treason against the state," the Major explained, "she soon confessed to everything, so we don't prosecute these people, too much press involvement and too many left wing liberals demanding that she's just a victim, so we had her sectioned under the Mental Health Act, the rest of her days will be spent climbing walls in Broadmoor with the rest of Britain's finest lunatics for company."

Mike shuddered; he couldn't think of a more depressing end to anyone's life; still if anyone deserved a fate worse than death it was that woman.

"OK then," said the Major, "I'm not going to try to talk you out of it Mike, I know you well enough to respect your wishes, I'll see to your discharge papers and all the paraphernalia this morning. Do you have an address where I can send everything?"

"Australia," came the reply.

Chapter 20 Harpenden High Street.

PC Evans had heard the all units call, but dismissed it almost immediately; it would be nice to get involved in some real action but that wasn't going to be today.

"Good morning, Sir," he said politely to Danny as he reached him. "I noticed your Car Tax is out of date, are you aware you could be prosecuted for failing to display your disc that is of course providing you actually have a current disc?"

Danny was now in control of his thoughts and figured he could soon blag his way out of this corner.

"I'm so sorry officer," he replied as humbly as he could. "My car wouldn't start this morning, and I was late for a meeting so grabbed the wife's keys and brought her car, the silly mare must have forgotten to tax the bloody thing, could I nip round to the Post Office now and get it done?"

"I'm sorry Sir, even if you did I'm still going to have to issue you with a ticket" came the reply.

"OK" said Danny, "that's fair enough, I'll give you my name and address and get on my way, if that's all right with you Constable."

PC Evans, still oblivious to the fact he was standing two meters from the man who had just robbed Barclays Bank in St Albans, agreed that would be fine.

"If I could just see some identification then, and you can get going."

Shit, thought Danny, one of the golden rules when you went out thieving was you never carried any identification or indeed any thing that could fall out of your pockets which could later incriminate you. Danny made a play of searching his pockets, and then looking surprised.

"This is so embarrassing, in my rush to get out I've left all my wallet and credentials in the other motor, and I've got no ID at all."

"Very well, Sir" said the officer, "If you give me your name and address I'll call it through to the centre, get it verified then you can get on your way."

Danny was starting to feel uneasy, but as long as he kept his cool he was still fine. There was absolutely nothing to tie him up with the robbery, in any case he could hardly drop this officer in broad daylight and make a run for it, no the best thing to do was hard nose it out. Danny gave the Constable his name and address down in Kent and PC Evans apologised for the inconvenience, stepped a few yards away, and radioed the general incident room at St Albans Police Station.

As is the case in all major crime the Police rarely solves these cases with detective work alone; most seasoned criminals know how to keep one step ahead of the chasing pack of police, no, what usually occurs is a lucky break, and then it's down to the detectives to recognise such incidents and act accordingly.

And so it was that on this particular morning in St Albans a lucky break materialised.

The Police Station was being graced by a legend of the Metropolitan Police, who had been invited to address the local force on major crime in the City of London, and how to prevent it.

Chief Superintendent Frank Carter had been preparing his seminar in the canteen when all hell broke loose, and the duty Sergeant Paul Ammonds had burst into the canteen and informed him of the robbery at the bank, apologising that he was going to have all his people out on the turf and the meeting would have to be postponed.

"Don't worry" said Frank as he was told the news, "Mind if I stick around though? I won't get in any one's way, and if I can help at all my day will be well spent." Inwardly he was quite pleased, public speaking was not his thing, and this felt a lot more exciting.

"Of course, Sir" answered the Sergeant. "You might feel comfortable in the incident room."

Frank Carter had made his way down to the incident room and found a hive of activity, the place was buzzing. As he stood in the corner, observing all around him, he overheard one of the switchboard operators commenting to her colleague:

"Bloody typical of Evans, we've got a major incident on our hands, and he's called in a no tax disc, so I've got to verify the owner of the car is who he says he is."

Frank laughed to himself, typical of today's police force; in his day he would have pulled that constable back in to look for the real criminals before the trail went cold.

"I know you're snowed under Shelia" replied the operator's colleague. "Give me his name and address

128

and I'll check it out."

"Cheers mate," Shelia replied "It's Danny Gallagher, Ivy cottage, Long Lane, Goudhurst, Kent."

Frank Carter froze. Danny fucking Gallagher, here on the manor, today of all days, never in a million years is this a coincidence. He leapt from his corner and instructed the operator to wait right there, he needed to think, and fast. He ran up the stairs, taking them three at a time, and into the duty Sergeant's office. Without knocking, he burst in. A group of senior CID officers were in a huddle, busily discussing their next moves.

"One of your PCs is only talking to a known blagger about a late Tax Disc, who happens to be on the patch," he blurted out.

The general hubbub ceased, everyone realised this could be the lucky break they needed.

"Right" said the officer in charge. "Find an excuse and let's get him in."

Frank Carter was now in his element, and he flew back downstairs to the incident room and took over the radio to PC Evans:

"Constable," he instructed in a very calm voice. "This is Frank Carter of the Flying Squad, I want you to listen carefully, stay calm and show no reaction to what I'm about to say." Frank continued: "I want you to explain to Mr Gallagher that the car in his possession has been reported stolen this morning, and until we ascertain who he is and to whom the car belongs, he should accompany you to the station where further enquiries will be made so we can eliminate him from the suspected theft of the car and clear up the matter. Apologise, and tell him it will probably be sorted by the time you both get here, do not spook him and be relaxed, can you handle that Constable?"

"Leave it to me Sir" replied the somewhat perplexed officer.

As Frank switched the microphone off another call came in from a member of the public. As Frank seemed to have taken charge, the operator turned directly to him.

"Excuse me Sir" she said, "it may be nothing but a local farmer has just reported a suspicious van which appears to have been abandoned up a small lane in Harpenden."

This was turning out to be a good day, thought Frank; first Gallagher appears in Harpenden then a dumped van, what next? Frank knew a lucky break when he got one and this was staring him right in the face.

"Tell the farmer to stay nearby, but on no account to go near the vehicle," he instructed. "How do I get there?" he demanded, and with that he flew out of the station, into his car and arrived in Harpenden as PC Evans and Danny were making their way to St Albans nick, in the "stolen" Honda, with the officer at the wheel.

As PC Evans opened the rears doors of the Police Station to show a very pensive Danny Gallagher into the building, Frank Carter was opening the rear doors of the abandoned van up the track in Harpenden and he was very pleased to find that, hidden under an old blanket, were three sawn off shotguns and three hand guns. Frank, being old school, knew exactly what he needed to do.

Frank returned to the station behind the wheel of the Renault van which he had hot-wired, fortunately the car park at the rear was deserted, apart from a couple of squad cars and the Honda with no tax.

Several minutes later Frank Carter entered the interview room that was housing Danny Gallagher.

"Afternoon, Danny" said Frank "Fancy meeting you here."

Danny couldn't disguise his astonishment, but nonetheless, in the time he had been alone in the interview room, he had convinced himself there was nothing tangible they could hold him for, even if they had discovered who he was.

"Goodness me, Mr Carter what a surprise, still that's a bit handy you being here and all that, can you tell the local plod who I am? Madge will be getting worried, or are you the new traffic warden?" he quipped.

"Of course I will Danny," replied Frank nonchalantly, "just a couple of questions first. What brings you up to this manor?"

Danny explained the reason for his being in the area, he was looking to buy a fruit and veg store and had heard there was one up for grabs in a prime location, so on a whim, he had driven up to have a look.

Frank just nodded with a wry smile that Danny found quite disconcerting.

"So Danny, can you confirm the Honda that our local Bobby stopped you with does in fact belong to you, or rather to Madge?" Frank asked. "And can you confirm that's the vehicle you drove from Kent in this morning?"

"That's absolutely right, Mr Carter" replied Danny. "Now do you think we could get on with whatever you need to do, so I can get going?" he asked with as much confidence as he could muster.

"Certainly, Danny, could we have a quick look at the vehicle first?" enquired Frank.

For the life of him Danny couldn't make out what game Carter was playing, but he needed to get out now, so he replied: "Of course, can I go then?"

"Yes you can, Danny, and I'm sorry to have inconvenienced you." Danny was starting too really worry now.

Frank led Danny out of the interview room and

along the corridor past the Sergeant's office. As they passed it, Frank, this time politely, knocked the door.

"Sorry to trouble you Sergeant," he said, "I'm about to send Mr Gallagher on his way, would you accompany us to his car, I just need to have a quick look around first?"

The Sergeant looked puzzled. *Why the fuck waste my time looking at this bloke's banger when the shit has hit the fan*, he thought, still he was a Chief Super, so not much he could say apart from, "Yes Sir."

The three men walked into the car park. Frank enquired if Danny had the keys, which he had, as PC Evans had given them to Danny once they had arrived at the station, after all the car wasn't impounded and Danny was hardly going to bolt for it.

"Just open up the boot please" asked Frank.

Dannys stomach flipped, did as he was requested and as the boot was raised, all three men saw there in the well of the car, three sawn off shotguns and three hand guns.

"I think," said Frank "You had better tell Madge you're going to be late."

Frank Carter had had one of the best days of his illustrious career He had apprehended a major villain, (the fact he had fitted him up with a cast iron piece of skulduggery was of no consequence), and certainly Frank didn't feel a tinge of remorse, he knew Danny was involved in the blag, and all Frank had done was a good old fashioned piece of Policing. However, best keep it to himself, he thought, in the old days he would have been the hero of the saloon bar and the whiskey chasers would not have stopped all night.

The criteria now was to get to Danny to spill the names of his accomplices. Frank was aware this was going to be no easy task. Danny, like himself, had been round the block on more than one occasion, and the only way to get him to cough was to offer him a carrot he couldn't refuse.

Firstly though, they needed to get Danny moved to a secure location, His team would by now have realised Danny had been collared, so there was always the possibility that they might have a go at getting him out of the Police Station; unlikely, but these were ruthless people. That had been established earlier in the day. So Frank had organised a local Magistrate to issue a warrant to remand Danny in custody that same night, and Danny was whisked off to Paddington Green Police Station, the highest secure nick in London and the Home Counties.

As for Danny, his world had fallen apart in those few short hours since the raid. He knew Carter had fitted him up, but he also knew the more he protested the harder it would go for him. He was also canny enough to know that he had some small bargaining power left, and that he was bang to rights with the shooters, but there was no direct evidence linking him with being on the blag- circumstantial, yes, but a good brief could sow doubt in a Jury's mind, and thank God that the British Judicial System did not accept circumstantial evidence. Things were bleak, but they could have been worse.

The following morning Frank Carter had his first, and as it happened last, interview with Danny.

Overnight Danny had been charged with armed robbery and various other offences all relating to the previous day. Danny had spoken first.

"I'm not going to fuck about, Carter, you bastard, this is the deal and I'm not negotiating. If I grass up anyone I think may have been involved in that blag, I'm dead, no ifs or buts, I'm destined for the pigs" (a well known method of disposing of unwanted bodies by the Essex pikies). He continued: "so I need twenty four hour protection, a new passport, a new identity and enough money to start a new life"

"Danny, in all honesty, I would think about your proposition, to me it would be worth getting those other three, you clear off and they're banged up for the rest of their natural, that's four dangerous bastards off the streets and where they belong. However this is the new world and the Chief Constable would have none of it, he's never done a days policing in his short life, he wouldn't get it, so there's no chance."

"OK then" said Danny "If that's the way it is, no deals, let's go to court and see what my Brief has to say to the Jury."

That wasn't exactly how Frank had hoped it would go, and he tried one last tactic.

"Then you'll be doing the bird for everyone," he threatened.

"So be it" was Danny final comment.

Chapter 21

St Albans Crown Court, 1 Month Later

The Honourable Mark Handford sat in residency for the trial of Crown v Gallagher. The Judge had been hand picked for this role by the Lord Chancellor. Mark, a previous Queen's Councillor and Crown Prosecutor, was known for his right wing views; he was a product of bygone days, and thought that young offenders would benefit from the birch, and more serious felons deported to a land they could do no harm in, the Arctic Circle for instance.

The criminal fraternity were well aware of his Honour's reputation; however, unlike a suspicious juror, they had no recourse to complain or object and have him changed. If they got him, it was just hard luck.

It was most unusual for a case of this magnitude to have come to court in such a quick time; the Director of Public Prosecutions had been under no illusion that it was in the public interest to have this one dealt with in the utmost haste, and he in turn had put the necessary pressure on the Crown Prosecution Service to fast track the legal paperwork to get Gallagher in the dock. There was some nervousness on the part of the prosecutors that a good brief might swing it for Gallagher; after all, apart from the shooters, the evidence was circumstantial. However, the orders had come way up from the top of the food chain, and so the case, such as it was, was ready.

Danny Gallagher was in remarkably good spirits considering the magnitude of the charges; he had the best defence lawyer in the business and was, quite frankly, expecting a not guilty verdict on all charges.

His mood changed somewhat as he was escorted from the holding cells into court- he knew of the Judge's reputation, so when one of his custodians mischievously whispered in his ear who the Judge was today, he inwardly groaned.

Danny stood in the dock and observed his surroundings; the public gallery was packed, mainly with the press, both local and national- this was a big case, and one the public at large would follow with interest. The court usher summoned the gathered ensemble to rise as the Honourable Mark Hanford made his way into the chamber. Fourteen charges were read out, and after each one Danny was asked how he pleaded. He replied, "Not guilty" to each one.

The Judge instructed the Prosecution to begin, but in a moment of madness Danny addressed the Judge:

"Excuse me, Your Honour" he said, "You are accusing me of all these grave crimes, of which I am innocent, and yet the one charge I am guilty of in this case you have not bothered to mention."

The judge was not impressed by this breach of protocol, nonetheless he spoke:

"And what might that be then? "

"Failing to display a current tax disc" Danny quipped.

A ripple of laughter broke out in the Courtroom, and Danny studiously watched who on the Jury laughed. They all did; he had broken the tension that the Jurors must have been feeling and he considered he had just made a very smart move .However; his Honour was not of the same opinion.

"Mr Gallagher, during the course of this trial you will speak when asked, and only then, one more interruption and you will be further charged with contempt of this court," he said slightly red faced.

For the next three days, witnesses came and went:

bank staff, the police, the public, forensic experts, PC Evans, the tractor driver and any one the Prosecution felt might add a blow to the nail they were driving into Danny's coffin.

At the end of the prosecution, it was Danny's lawyer's turn to address the jury. His speech was eloquent and well presented, he disseminated all the evidence that had gone before, and demonstrated the thread running through the prosecutor's case was one of circumstance- there was not one single piece of evidence that put Danny at the scene of the robbery, and therefore under the law of the land Danny could not be found guilty. The members of the Jury might believe Danny was guilty, but it was not their job to second guess, they had to know Danny was involved by the evidence presented to them, and this had not been the case.

The Right Honourable Mark Handford summed up, and in his usual jaundiced way, just fell short of instructing the Jury to return a guilty verdict on all counts. With that, he instructed the eight men and four women of the Jury to retire to the ante room and discuss the case. When they had reached a unanimous verdict, they would inform the court Bailiff, who would bring them back to deliver their decision.

Before Danny was taken back to the cells, he was allowed a few minutes with his brief.

"Well, Michael" he asked "What do you reckon?"

"In the bag, dear boy," came the reply. "I watched their faces as I spoke, and I've been reading Juries for two decades, and they're not sure. Danny you'll be a free man by sunset."

Those in the know at the Courthouse were confident this was going to be a long haul; they were fully expecting a couple of over nighters, followed by a return of the Jury failing to reach a unanimous decision, and then being ordered to return to their deliberations to consider a majority guilty verdict at best. So when after barely three hours, the Courthouse tanoy announced the Jury in the trial of Danny Gallagher was returning, and all participants were to return to court no 1 immediately, it was quite a surprise.

With all seated, the court usher instructed the foreman of the Jury to stand.

"Have you reached a verdict on all fourteen counts?" he enquired of the foreman.

"We have, sir," came the reply.

"And are you unanimous on all counts?" he asked

"We are," the young lady representing the Jury replied.

"In that case, I will read out the charges and after each one you should reply either 'guilty', or 'not guilty', is that clear?"

And with that concluded, the bailiff began reading out the charges- one by one came the reply: "Not guilty."

The Bailiff had reached the twelfth charge of which the not guilty verdict had been delivered. Danny was beaming like the proverbial Cheshire cat, and so he should be, he was home and dry.

The bailiff spoke: "The thirteenth charge, carrying firearms for unlawful reasons, how do you find the defendant?"

"Guilty" the foreman replied,

"And the last charge, the shortening of a shot gun for unlawful reason, how do you find the defendant?"

"Guilty" the young woman answered.

Danny was in a daze, so nearly home and dry. Fuck it, he thought, but shouldn't be too long a stretch, he barely heard the Judge thank and then dismiss the Jury.

It took several minutes for the courtroom to quieten down. The press were laying bets on what Danny

138

would get, and the prosecutors' were in deep conversation. It took his Lordship several moments of banging his gavel on the desk to bring the place to order.

The honourable Judge placed his half glasses on the end of his nose, not a good sign for the accused or as in this case the guilty. His huge bushy eyebrows had returned to their normal position, having nearly gone into orbit as he had listened incredulously to that stupid woman pronouncing Gallagher not guilty.

With the court room now silent, the Judge began, "Danny Gallagher, you are a hardened criminal with a history of violence, and the Jury have found you not guilty on all major charges in this case. However, the two charges you have been found guilty of remain extremely serious." His honour was at his sanctimonious best. "Therefore, on the charge of carrying unlicensed firearms, I see no reason other than to impose the maximum sentence, seven years imprisonment."

Even the hard nosed hacks winced; the judge was living up to his reputation.

"On the charge of shortening a shot gun, once again there is no reason other than to impose the maximum sentence, seven years imprisonment."

Once again, a stunned court room were shocked by the severity of the sentence. Danny was working out mentally what this meant in terms of actual imprisonment, and he'd concluded he would serve less than four years, just about manageable, when the judge spoke again:

"Furthermore, the sentences are to run consecutively. Court adjourned, take him down, officers."

This time there was an audible gasp from nearly the entire contingent of number one court. The judge had effectively sentenced Danny to fourteen years, unbelievable, consecutive sentences were unheard of in this day and age, but part of the judicial system which could be used if a judge saw enough reason to justify it. Danny hadn't registered what had just happened, he wondered why the congregation were looking so shell shocked, and then it dawned on him, that satanic monster had effectively sent him down for life. He'd be over seventy when he got out, oh my God, his stomach turned a somersault and his bowels loosened.

Later that evening, the Honourable Mark Handford was sitting in a cubicle of the Hare and Hounds public house, a quiet country pub on his way home. There were no other patrons at this early hour and the judge, sipping a large brandy, was feeling pleased with himself.

Chief Inspector Frank Carter entered the pub, spotted the Judge in his corner, and made his way across. Frank Carter was a man's man, one of the boys, after all was said and done; he had a begrudging respect for the villains he had spent a lifetime chasing, but this man sitting before him he despised. He knew his type, members of the upper echelon of the establishment, people who believed the law was theirs to administer as they saw fit, but not there for them to follow; these people believed they were immune to the rules and regulations that the rest of society had to follow, and to a large extent this was true. When these people transgressed they would expect their misdemeanours to be swept aside, they were practically invincible.

"I trust our business is satisfactorily concluded, and the matter closed Inspector," the Judge said.

Frank could barely conceal his contempt of the man.

The story was that the judge was a little too fond of underage boys. The Vice Squad were aware of his behaviour, and even had a dossier on him which included several explicit photos which would incriminate even this great man. Of course, in the normal path of events, if the judge had merely been Joe Public he would already have been doing some very nasty porridge with the paedophiles and perverts in the Scrubs, but he was too well connected, had too many friends in the right places, and too many of those friends shared the same tastes as the judge.

So Frank, who had been told about the dossier from one of his many friends in Vice, had borrowed the photos and paid the judge a visit two weeks prior to the trial. For maximum effect, he had called on the Judge at home and been made most welcome. As the Judge's wife had retired to the kitchen to make the men some coffee, Frank, not known for his subtle ways, has produced the photos and without a word thrown them over the Persian carpet in the Judge's sitting room. This had the desired effect. Mark Handford absolutely panicked, and just about managed to gather the pornographic material up before his wife re entered the room. He asked her if she could leave them alone whilst they discussed an up and coming case, and hissed after she had left: "What the hell do you want, you're not going to arrest me or you would have done so by now, so this must be blackmail, how much?"

Frank grinned. "You have no idea, you perverted ponce, here's what I want. I want you to make sure you're presiding in a trial due in St Albans in two weeks, it is the blag at Barclays, St Albans The defendant stands a chance of getting off, but we know him, so you've got to influence the Jury. This bastard Gallagher's got to go down one way or another, so you have to ensure he does, the deal is this, he gets twelve years or more, you get the photos back. Under twelve the photos go to the DPP, or worse, the News of The World, and believe me it will happen."

Frank didn't give the Judge chance to remonstrate. He apologised to the Judge's wife, but some thing urgent had come up back at the Yard, so the coffee would have to wait for another time. Frank shut the front door on his way out,

"What a lovely man," commented Celia Handford as Frank left.

Back in the pub Mark Handford was getting cross now. "Look here, Carter, I've done my bit, I gave him fourteen years, now you either give me the photos or you can consider your career over, I'm a personal friend of your Chief Constable" he said smugly.

With this, Frank rose from his chair and placed a two pound coin on the table.

"What's this?" the judge asked angrily.

"I suggest you purchase an early edition of this Sunday's News of The World" was Frank's reply.

Chapter 22

Jock Wallace

Since Jock and Mike had arrived back in Hereford, things hadn't gone well for Jock. To make matters worse, with Mike's departure to Australia, Jock had felt very much alone He had effectively lost the three mates he had lived with for the last six months. He knew nothing else other than the Army, so unlike Mike, who he felt a certain envy of, he had stayed on at Sterling Lines but his heart wasn't in it. As much as he tried, his motivation was gone, therefore it came as no surprise when he was summoned to a meeting one morning with the CO.

"Jock, we have to discuss your future with us," Major Morley started. "You must be aware that since you returned from that fracas in Pakistan you have not been up to speed, in fact, Jock, to be brutal, you would not be accepted into this unit on your current performance. You would be a liability on any operation we might have to handle in the near future, and I can't allow that. As much as it pains me, I have no alternative other than to recommend you are Returned To Unit immediately."

In an attempt to soften the blow, the Major added, "But of course you will be free to reapply to the Regiment whenever you feel ready."

Jock was devastated- all serving members of the SAS had started their army life in normal regiments, they then applied to the SAS and if successful transferred to the elite troop. Only in the initial training months were applicants RTUd, this was acceptable, but not after ten years; no, as far as Jock was concerned this was it, his army life was finished, over and out.

Jock knew the Major well enough to know any sort of pleading would do him no good at all.

"I'm gutted, boss," he said. "But there's no way I can go back to being a squaddie, I'm out."

"I'm really sorry, Jock," continued the Major "If there's any thing we can do to help you in Civvy Street, let me know," and with that the chief stood and outstretched his right arm, which Jock accepted, and showed him the door.

The next few months were not kind to Jock. Initially, he travelled back to his native Glasgow and tried numerous jobs. Employers were keen to take on an ex SAS trooper, so Jock had no problem finding gainful employment, but he couldn't handle the mundane life of Civvy Street- the petty rules and regulations were too much. Jock's skills as a mechanic were not appreciated either, he had to learn the philosophy of his new way of life: a good job was a botched job, take as much of the customer's money as you could, for as little as you get away with. This was an alien world for Jock, who started to drift back into his old haunts of Glasgow's East End, taking solace in the bottom of a glass. Before long, Jock started mixing with the wrong crowd. Glasgow's East End was still a viper's nest of petty villains, pimps and prostitutes. Territorial gangs ruled, and a fair share of real bad guys inhabited the place. It was no surprise that Jock felt more at home in this environment than that of the legitimate workplace, and the local hoods soon recognised that Jock possessed some unusual talents which they could deploy.

Jock became a doorman at a particularly nasty dive in a particularly nasty area, just off Argyle Street. He regularly found himself facing the local wannabes in street brawls and skirmishes within the club, and he always found himself coming out on top. What Jock possessed, along with his ability to keep the house in order, was intelligence, unusual for this type of work, so it was no surprise when the owner called him to the back room one night.

"Jock, I've been watching you since you started here," he said in his deep Scottish brogue. "And I have to say the way you've kept the door and sorted out the trouble makers, I'm prepared to take a chance on you, fucking hell, we all started with nothing round here, so how would you fancy being the new manager?"

"Well that would be just fine, Mr Donaldson," replied Jock.

"Good," came the reply. "Let me put the cards on the table then, you're not stupid Jock, no doubt you've seen what goes on around here, and it not all Kosher, so I'm going to pay you two grand a week For that, you manage the club and when you're not doing that you're minding my back."

"Yup, I can handle that, it's very generous, thank you Mr Donaldson," Jock replied.

"One last thing, I've noticed you like a wee dram a bit too often- as of now, you're off the sauce."

The weeks passed, and Jock immersed himself in his new employment. It was to his liking- plenty of excitement, long hours and perks of which Major Morley would definitely not have approved.

One Sunday morning, when all was quiet, Mr Donaldson invited Jock out to his country house, at Greenock, overlooking the Firth of Clyde. They walked out in the gardens, watching the few container ships that still made the journey into Port Glasgow. Mr Donaldson turned to Jock.

"Jock, you have done better than I could have hoped, nothing seems to faze you, so I want you to go down south and do a little pick up for me."

"No problem" replied Jock. "Can you tell me

more?" he asked.

"That's why you're here, in the privacy of my home" came the reply.

Jock, being quick, realised this was something out of the ordinary. In the time he had been working for Donaldson, he had handled drugs and illegal women, and even firearms, but all this was done as a matter of course from the club.

Mr Donaldson continued: "I can see, Jock, you've realised this is a bit special and it is, so there's twenty large ones in it for you. I want you to go down to Kent, buy a van, then rendezvous with a plane that will be dropping a couple of large bags of dope in a remote field just off the coast. You're there to pick up the drugs and get back up here with them- simple, really."

"So why do we have to go all the way down into England to pick it up, wouldn't it be safer if the plane dumped it round here?" asked Jock.

"Good question," came the reply, "The simple reason is that the plane's coming in over the English Channel low, so by the time it's picked up on radar it will be back out again, and away from British air space, and, more to the point, if it flew all the way up here it would need to refuel and that can't happen. One other thing, Jock, there shouldn't be a problem but you had better go tooled up, just in case."

Jock considered this, and then asked: "When do I go?"

"The drop's three am Wednesday morning, so come back to the house and I'll find you a decent shooter, and you can be off."

The following Tuesday morning found Jock in Folkestone High Street, bartering for a reasonable Mercedes Sprinter van, with a spotty youth who was so disinterested there was no problem he would ever recall Jock, never mind remembering selling Jock the van.

Jock thought if he told him the reason for the purchase,that might get his attention. With the van acquired, Jock drove south, along the coast road towards Dymchurch. He needed to acquaint himself with the terrain and the pick up point; the first time since Jock had left the army that his specialised training was being put to good use.

Jock decided to spend the first half of that night in the back of the van, and go over the plans one last time. He had the co- ordinates of the drop memorised- he was to park the van on the edge of the field facing south. As the plane approached, Jock was to flash the van lights three times. The plane would fly over at no more than one hundred feet and discharge the two sacks of drugs in the middle of the field, Jock would then give the plane five minutes, and if all was clear, he would drive into the field, load the two hessian sacks, and twenty minutes later be on the M20 heading north, twenty grand richer.

At two am that Wednesday morning, Jock was in position. He had left the van, and was surveying the perimeter of the field on foot. No one would have seen him; it was what he did best. Jock was comfortable that he was alone; the only sound was that of the sea, breaking waves less than a kilometre away.

At precisely three am Jock heard the sound of a low flying aircraft, probably a Cessna, approaching. This was it- he flashed his lights, and before he knew it the plane was passing directly overhead, climbing steeply and banking to its right. Even with Jock's night glasses, it had all been so quick he didn't even know if the illegal cargo had been jettisoned successfully.

After five minutes nothing stirred, so Jock started up the motor, and under cover of darkness made his way out into the middle of the field. After a couple of precautionary circles, he spotted the contraband and pulled up with the back doors next to the sacks. Jock loaded the goods into the back, and tentatively made his way back to the outskirts of the field. Just as he was about to put the van lights on, all hell broke loose. From nowhere, a huge spotlight illuminated half the field; Jock was the proverbial rabbit caught in the headlights, but the difference was this rabbit was armed and dangerous. A loud hailer broke the silence.

"This is Customs and Excise, leave the vehicle and lay flat on the ground, do not move or we will open fire" came the instruction.

Jock didn't go into a panic, worse, he went into regression, and he was back in the Hindu Kush and these were the Warlords of Northern Pakistan. Without hesitation, he removed the Colt automatic from the glove box, exited the vehicle and opened fire. The lights from the vehicle went out, and Jock heard two simultaneous screams- with luck he had caused so much confusion he could still get out of there. Jock had to drive right past the Customs and Excise van to get out of the field. He saw two officers lying motionless, and without a second thought, he gunned the van down the lane he had already identified as an escape route-with luck he could still make it. He rounded a bend, the motorway lights were visible, but to his horror blocking his way were two police vans and several officers who were obviously marksmen, and there was too much firepower in this group for Jock to do any thing. He couldn't do a u turn, the lane was too narrow, reversing was out of the question; these were trained shooters and he sensed they would open fire any second, so he stopped the van, very very slowly got out and laid on the cold tarmac face down.

Three months later it took Dover Crown Court less than two days to convict Jock of the murder of two Customs and Excise officers, as well as possession of two hundredweight of cannabis. It took the presiding Judge less than two minutes to sum up and sentence Jock to a double count of life imprisonment, to serve a minimum of eighteen years.

Jock Wallace had fallen a long way in a very short time,

Chapter 23

HMP Prison Parkhurst A Wing

Built in 1805, Parkhurst Prison enjoyed a certain infamy as Britain's toughest prison. In recent years, the prison has housed some of the country's most notorious criminals, including Ian Brady the Moors murderer, the Kray Twins and the Yorkshire Ripper, Peter Sutcliffe. Various attempts at escape have taken place over the years; the most recent occurred in 1995 when three prisoners- two murderers and a blackmailer- made it out, only to be apprehended four days later in a garden shed in Ryde, Isle of Wight. Therein lies the reason why the prison houses so many dangerous felons- to escape not only requires the guile to get out of the confines of the prison, but once on the outside there is still the problem of getting off the island.

It remains a common misunderstanding of the general public that prison life, and the regime that it entails, is an easy life- for those within the system, nothing could be farther from the truth. The reality of being locked up, usually with one or two other prisoners not of your choice, is a living hell and nowhere more so than on The Isle of Wight, where the sense of isolation felt by the inmates is heightened by the geography of being divorced from mainland Britain.

Prison life, like civilian life, like the animal kingdom, develops a hierarchy within its community; the strong survive at the expense of the weak, and so gangs evolve with the strongest leading the pack, and the gangs that run the inside of the Prisons are the most feral of all.

To survive the ordeal of lengthy incarceration, all

inmates must pin their colours to one of the gangs; it is nothing more than self preservation, that is, unless of course you are one of the few individuals that can survive without the comfort of a group. These people, who didn't need the security of gang membership, or the patronage of a gang master, were usually the hardest inmates; those who were doing the longest sentences, for the worst crimes, and who were considered the most resilient to the penal system and they could be found on A Wing.

John Illes, a.k.a the Mouse, was one of these people. There were two reasons Mouse was on A wing- initially, simply because as one of the leading figures in the Brinks Mat job he was considered highly dangerous, and secondly, since his incarceration, his arresting officer one Frank Carter, Flying Squad, had let it leak, in the appropriate quarters, that the great blagger and hard man John Illes had offered to turn queen's evidence against his fellow conspirators to obtain early or immediate release, what is known in prison parlance as a grass. The Prison Governor had decided that, as fearsome as Mouse's reputation was, and indeed the respect shown to him by the rest of the prison community, there would always be the chance of some young buck trying to enhance their reputation by causing considerable harm to Mouse, so Mouse was on A wing as much to keep him out of harm's way as to keep him under special surveillance.

Mouse occupied Cell forty nine on the wing. He was the single occupant, and had been since his arrival. His visits had dropped off since he had instructed Danny Gallagher to employ the hitman to gain revenge for the double crossing following his sentence. John had done the usual thing since being locked up, and had even gained a degree from the Open University in medieval history. However, the one thing that occupied his mind above all else was the thought of escape; and he could not come to terms, like some, with seeing out his sentence, or even accepting his future in the prison.

It was a normal Tuesday morning in the prison the wing was on lock down, and Mouse was sitting on his mattress when he heard the wardens walking along the steel infrastructure that constituted the floor, talking to what was probably a new inmate. A new inmate always caused great interest amongst the prison fraternity, who could it be, what have they done, were they known, what stories could they tell at recreation. Mouse was no exception and he went to his door and peaked out of the small hatch, in an attempt to catch a glimpse of the poor bastard.

As Danny Gallagher walked past Mouse's cell, escorted and flanked by two screws, Mouse nearly shouted in astonishment and amazement, but incredibly he kept his cool and watched as Danny was led down the wing and shown his hotel room about ten cells down. For the rest of the day all Mouse could contemplate was: was this a good thing or not that Danny was now going to be sharing the wing with him?

The next morning at breakfast, Mouse waited for Danny to join the queue of hungry inmates. As Danny took up position, looking to all intents and purpose like the new boy, which he was, Mouse tucked in behind him, tapped him on the right side and moved to the left, Danny turned one way then the other.

"Mouse!" he exclaimed in shock. "Jesus, you made me jump."

Both men realised the sense of déjà-vu going back to that meeting in Spain in 84, and burst out laughing, although the circumstances were far different, and neither man had anything to make them smile.

So Danny and Mouse were reunited, and spent all their free time, as little as it was, together, huddled in a corner in the recreation hall. Their conversation was initially focused on the good old days, but as the weeks passed by and they ran out of stories, the conversation became more sporadic and maudlin. Eventually they began to discuss their circumstances, and together they agreed, some how- God knew how, they had to get out of this shit hole.

One particular morning, Mouse was saying to Danny: " The fucking stupid thing is, I can get my hands on a million quid, more if necessary, surely a million quid would get us out of here, for fucks sake we could hire a small army for that."

"Yup" Danny said, "I think, Mouse, we need to start putting our feelers out, we both know plenty of people on the outside, at least we can start moving in the right direction, for a million quid we could, as you say, get a tank to come through these walls and Bruce fucking Willis to fly us out."

Both men grinned, but in their earnest plotting they had failed to notice Prisoner 080374 passing by within earshot, and he had heard enough to realise these two were not only talking about busting out, but deadly serious.

During the next couple of weeks, Prisoner 080374 kept a watchful eye on Mike and Danny. He could lip read a bit, and was able to verify his earlier suspicions that these two villains were hell bent on jumping ship, and as it happened, so was he. It was now a problem of approaching the two conspirators. How could he tell these two bank robbers, who thought nothing of maiming anyone who got in their way, that he had been listening in on their conversations about escaping, and that he had a very good plan as long as they took him with them? In the end, Prisoner 080374 decided he had to bite the bullet- the worst that could happen would be a serious assault in the near future, but actually even

153

that was highly unlikely, as he was more than capable of handling himself, and what's more, over the time of his incarceration, he had proved to be an inmate not to be messed with.

It was a couple of days later that he plucked up the courage to approach Mouse. It was that time between the evening meal and lockdown when prisoners have the choice between recreation or staying in their cells with the doors open, so that they can to some extent talk between themselves, a privilege only allowed on A wing.

Mouse was sitting alone in his cell when the door was knocked.

"Mr Illes," the prisoner started, "Could I talk with you on a highly delicate subject? It's quite likely that you will be extremely angry before I finish, and that's fair enough, but all I ask is you don't interrupt when I'm speaking, you hear me out, and then if you want to give me a good hiding I wont complain."

Mouse was interested, what harm could this bloke do? If he didn't like what he was saying he'd give him a good kicking alright, way before he'd finished if necessary.

"Pull the door to, but keep a lookout for any screws, and this had better be good." he said.

Prisoner 030874, ex SAS trooper Jock Wallace, began: "Mr Illes, I have reason to believe you would dearly like to escape from this penitentiary, like every single person in here, me included, however I believe the difference between you and the rest is that you have both the resolve and the money, that you will need to make this happen."

Mouse raised his eyebrows, but was too inquisitive by now to toss this bloke Wallace out.

" I was in the SAS for ten years," continued Jock, " In that time, I committed as many crimes as you

154

probably have, the difference being I was doing it for King and Country, whereas you were doing it for personal gain. I've murdered people in cold blood and undoubtedly witnessed more violence for the safety of the realm than you have in your life of crime."

"Your point is?" Mouse was starting to get agitated.

"My point is, that an SAS soldier is not a normal soldier, we are trained to be fearless fighters, and we are trained as experts in munitions, covert warfare, hostage taking, explosives and many ways to kill hostiles. In short, with my help I believe I can offer you the best possible chance of getting out of here, but I've got to come as well."

"So what you're saying is, with your expertise as a SAS soldier, you could break us out of here?" asked Mouse.

"Not exactly," replied Jock. "But I know a man that can."

"Who is this person, why is he is so special, and how do we get him on board?" enquired Mouse, by now hooked.

Jock let out a big sigh. " The person is someone I worked with in the unit, they were, are, the best in the business, highly trained in the art of organising recovery of assets, that's people, from the most hostile places on Earth. Extraction is a skill taught to few but the most trusted soldiers, you wouldn't know this but training an individual or unit to rescue people has involved the breaking into various establishments in the UK that the brass think are impenetrable. The man I'm talking about has to my knowledge already successfully broken into and out of several high security areas, such as Aldermaston Weapons Facility, The Tate Gallery and most significantly Dartmoor prison, and that's just training, it's a hell of a lot harder out there in the field, believe me, I've been with him on some real scary missions."

"So," said Mouse "Suppose I believe all this, you reckon your man, presumably with your help, could get us out of here, why would he want to do that? You must be pretty close mates or some thing."

"One million pounds" Jock replied, looking Mouse dead in the eye.

Mouse was silent, was this bloke shitting him, no reason to, was he a nutter, no, Mouse was wise enough to have assessed everyone on the wing, and he had this bloke Jock down as a loner, but a quiet type, not to be picked on, which was good in Mouse's book. After due consideration Mouse spoke:

"Right , there's nothing to lose by talking to your man , get him a Visiting Order to come in, you talk to him, and I'll give you the questions I want answering before he gets here, and then we'll see how it goes."

Jock looked suitably distressed before he spoke.

"That's the one problem, we had a mission go badly wrong, and so he retired. I'm not sure of his address, but if we could locate him the prospect of one million pounds and the thought of helping an old mate out of a deep hole will, I hope, be enough to persuade him to work out a plan to get us out of here."

"No problem," said Mouse, "I have plenty of people who are experts at finding people, even those that don't want to be found. I also have people who can be very persuasive in convincing people to do as I ask," He said menacingly, "Just tell me where he was last seen and we'll find him."

"Australia," Jock replied.

Chapter 24

Cell 49, A wing, 2 Weeks Later

Since the evening when Jock Wallace had visited him with his life changing proposals, Mouse had been busy. Mouse spent the first night lying on his bunk going through what needed to be done. The logistics problems were huge, and the facts were that somewhere in Australia was a man, retired, who needed to be found, persuaded to return to England, and then to devise and execute a plan that would get Mouse, Danny and Jock out of this prison, off the Island, and ensconced somewhere the authorities could neither find them nor touch them. The what ifs were enormous, but that didn't deter Mouse; one way or another he would get his man to do what was required. If this guy was as good as the sweat was telling him, why not? The first morning after Jock's visit Mouse had already made some decisions. The escape plan, although in its embryonic stage, was underway.

Mouse had recognised that the modern day Prison Warden was more than just a janitor, especially on A Wing, where the screws were trained in psychological behavioural patterns, so he had figured out a new relationship with Jock would not go unnoticed, a file note would be made and maybe some smart arse up the line would want to know why John Illes had befriended some no hoper thug from Glasgow. So at breakfast, Mouse had whispered in Jock's ear that he was going to do some "work" on the project, and that it was best if they weren't seen talking together. He told Jock to narrow down the field of search, or ideally come up with an address for the man in Australia, it shouldn't be too hard, after all, he wasn't on the run or anything, and he must surely have left a forwarding address with someone.

John then joined Danny for breakfast, looking across the table he said: "We're on the move, mate." Danny just looked very hard at Mouse, who looked back with that old twinkle that had been missing of late. *Fucking hell, he's serious,* Danny realised.

That evening in Danny's cell, Mouse filled him in about the previous night's conversation. Danny listened intently, just nodding his acknowledgement occasionally. Eventually Mouse finished.

"What do you think?" he asked Danny.

"Well, I'm not going to say no, that's for sure," replied Danny. "But we don't know this sweat from Adam, he could be full of shit, or worse the real deal, who could get us out then burn us for the million, or he could be our salvation, so we run with him, for now."

Mouse agreed. "So here's what we do then," he declared. "The Jock will track down this geezer, Mike Tobin, or at least give us a bearing where he might be. You, Danny, will get hold of someone we trust, say Dave Ward, and get us the lowdown on this Jock Wallace, and tell him we want every detail no matter how small. I will get Cathy to come in next week, tell her I need to talk to Niall Penny and Richard Sykes, brief her why, and take it from there."

The two characters Mouse was talking about were gangland enforcers, and their expertise was in convincing people who were playing up, one way or another, to step back into line. The tools of their trade were knives and sulphuric acid, and their reputation preceded them wherever they were asked to go.

"Penny and Sykes don't fuck about Mouse," replied Danny, "are you sure? I presume they're going to be going down to Oz to convince our man breaking us out of here is a good thing for him?"

"Well" said Mouse "The place is so far away, I could send Cathy, who would be charming, offer him a million quid, and bobs your uncle, he says yes, no problem, but if he doesn't want to play, there's fuck all Cathy can do or say, so I'd have to send the boys out then in any case, they can be polite when they need to."

"Yeah, and vicious when they want to be, so if this guy in Oz says no to the money, then the boys will convince him otherwise." commented Danny.

"That's about the size of it" Mouse replied.

"Well, from what I know about the SAS, he isn't gonna be no push over, if the money doesn't appeal." Danny said.

"Danny," said Mouse, "this is maybe our best chance of getting out of here, it would be far better if he agreed willingly, but if he is the best man to get us free then whatever it takes will be worth it. The boys aren't stupid, they will understand strong arm tactics are to be used only as a last resort, so let's keep our distance from here on in, we will reconvene in a couple of weeks when I've seen Cathy and you've got the low down from Dave on the Jock. The Jock will hopefully have tracked down this Mike Tobin, and then we can plan the next moves, fair enough?"

"Fair enough" replied Danny.

Two weeks later, just before lockdown, John and Danny were sitting in John's cell.

Mouse spoke first. "So, Danny, let's see where we're at. Cathy came in just after we last spoke, she's spoken with Penny and Sykes, they know the score, they also figured out we're desperate, they want fifty thousand up front to bring Tobin back, whether they have to persuade him or he comes of his own free will, I've agreed, it's daylight robbery, but we have no choice, have you got any information on the Jock yet?"

Danny replied, " Sure have, Dave's done a proper

159

job, obviously we had to have a guarded conversation as we spoke on the phone, but the upshot is he got kicked out of the Army after something really big he was involved in went tits up, he then got mixed up with some real bad dudes in Scotland, this cumulated in him shooting two Customs officers, which is why he's here, but what Wardy found out that he's well thought of, the way he handled himself through out the whole affair, the word is he's his own man, and not to be messed with."

"Right," said Mouse " that confirms what I thought, I caught up with him this morning, he's found out that this mate of his is living and working in a little place called Port Douglas, which is up in Queensland. It won't be hard for the boys to find him, so I reckon our next move is, I get Cathy to pull fifty large ones, get the boys on their way, and as soon as they get him back here he can have a couple of weeks to suss things out then come in, and tell Jock how and when we go"

"I'm going to sleep well tonight." was all Danny could think of to say.

Chapter 25

Queensland, Australia

Mike Tobin had arrived in Australia two years previously. He had had no real plans, or even any idea where he might live on the huge continent. He did have a big bank balance so he could suit himself for a couple of years at least, or until the local authorities started asking questions. So quite simply, Mike had booked himself the first available flight out of Heathrow and found himself in the town of Cairns. He found a reasonable long let, hired a camper van, and began to explore Northern Queensland hoping something might turn up, and as luck had it, it did.

One bright morning, Mike had driven out of town, heading north up the Cook Highway, when he spotted an old guy on the side of the road obviously looking for a ride. Mike stopped and enquired where he was going.

"Heading up to Port Douglas, about forty miles north," replied the grateful passenger.

"OK," Mike said, I'm heading North, I'll drop you off."

The two men started a general conversation, and it turned out the passenger, whose name was Charlie Allington, was, like so many in Australia, from the British Isles. He had emigrated in the 1960s from his home in Bishops Stortford, paid ten pounds for the privilege, and set up a business in the town they were heading.

"So what do you do?" enquired Mike.

Charlie took a deep breath. "It's a long story son, but back in those days this place was the Outback, no one came apart from the occasional Black fellas on walkabout, so I worked the mines, then as the town began to grow, I worked on the construction of the new hotels that were shooting up. I'd made a lot of money down the mines, so I was always looking for an opportunity to invest, this was the country for opportunists and I wanted to be part of it."

"Go on." said Mike, fascinated by the man's story.

"So, as the town grew, we suddenly realised we were sitting on a gold mine, and hadn't realised it."

"So you went back down the mines?" asked Danny.

The old guy laughed aloud. " No, what I meant was a metaphorical gold mine, sitting just off the coast, none of us from these parts had even thought about it, and it's almost unbelievable now, you would know it as The Great Barrier Reef. But back in those days it was just a bloody nuisance for the fishing boats to navigate, they were forever getting their nets snagged and maybe twenty boats a year were lost by ripping their bottoms out. Anyhow, people started arriving, initially from the towns down south, looking for the weather, and then they got more adventurous and wanted to go out to the Reef, to see for themselves, so I went and bought myself a charter boat, went all the way to Sydney for it, then sailed it back here, and that was that. I didn't even have to advertise, just stood out on the dock each morning and within the hour, every day, it was full, twenty eager holiday makers all wanting to see the wonders of the sea. Over the years we've had to move with the times, it started when people were happy enough just to take a few a photos, but of course now they want to get in the ocean and dive, so we offer all that malarkey on the boat, we could have expanded like some round here, but what we got does us fine."

"When you say we," Mike asked "Is it your family, or do you have a partner?"

Charlie shook his head. "No, it's just me and my daughter. I lost my wife a few years ago, she got stung by one of the jellyfish round here and we never got her to the hospital in time, so it's just the two of us now. Anyhow," he said swiftly changing the subject, "what about you. young fella, what's your story?"

Mike thought about the question, it would be good to unburden some of life, even onto a stranger. "Have you got a couple of hours spare?" he enquired.

"Actually, I have." said Charlie, "So why don't you come and have some lunch down on the berth, I'm sure there's a couple of cold beers I could find, if you're interested. Jane, that's my daughter, is doing the trip today, so I'll show you the boat when she returns."

"Sounds good," came the reply.

So Mike and Charlie drove into Port Douglas. Charlie took the opportunity to point out the charm of the place as they drove along the ocean boulevard, explaining that at this point the Pacific Ocean had given way to the Coral Sea. The beach was known as the four mile beach, for obvious reasons, and just beyond the horizon lay the Great Barrier Reef. Port Douglas is a spit of land that goes nowhere, the road out is the same road in. At the top of town they turned left along the main street, Macrossan Street, bustling with people along the old- fashioned boardwalks. Tables and chairs lined the footway, and the chic boutiques that were interspersed between the hostelries gave the air of a very laid back, but upmarket town.

Leaving the precinct behind, they turned again and this time the ocean gave way to a river, or creek. Charlie explained that it was called Dickens Creek and it was a subsidiary of the Mossman River. This was the side of the town where all the boats were moored, safe from the odd cyclone that would blow in from the Coral Sea. Charlie shortly turned into a public car park, which led them through into the boat yard; there were few boats moored at this time of day and they pulled up alongside a berth housing a small kiosk, and displaying a For Sale sign. Mike was curious.

"Is this your berth?" he enquired.

"Sure is" replied Charlie.

"What's with the For Sale sign?" Mike asked.

Charlie looked wistfully at Mike. " Well, it's like this, I've been doing this for over twenty years, and I can honestly say I've enjoyed every single moment, every day meeting new people, all of them excited in anticipation of going over the Reef, that rubs off on you."

Charlie opened a couple of bottles of Victoria Bitter, handing one to Mike he continued, " But unfortunately over the years the motion of the sea has caused the lower part of my back to wear out, and some days out on the reef I wonder if I'll make it back with the pain, that's life, so I've made enough money to live more than comfortably for the rest of my days, and I'm going to stay round these parts, so there would be nothing stopping me going out there occasionally if the new owner didn't mind."

Both men sat in the easy chairs that were permanently placed by the side of the kiosk. The dock was nearly deserted; the sky was that huge expanse of ice blue only found in Australia. Mike began to tell Charlie his story, leaving out the more graphic details. Two more beers were opened, and Mike fell silent.

"Something troubling you, son?" asked Charlie

"How much did you say you were asking for the boat?" Mike asked.

"Well I didn't, but it's not a secret. One hundred thousand Aussie dollars," came the reply.

Mike was a good judge of character, and for a few seconds he looked into Charlie's eyes.

"Done."

Charlie looked stunned, but things like this

happened in these parts Both men grinned simultaneously and extended their right arms, deal secured.

Two more tinnies were cracked open in the way of a celebration, and the conversation turned to the logistics of the sale. As the sun began its descent across the creek, a long range, ocean going trawler, technically know as a passagemaker rounded the headland, and made its way sedately through the Marina. Mike commented to Charlie, "Nice looking boat."

"That's a relief" said Charlie "It's yours."

The sixty footer was expertly reversed into the berth, and Charlie and Mike both greeted the passengers warmly as they alighted with photos and stories to take back home. As the last of the passengers left, the skipper, Jane, Charlie's daughter, made her way to the front of the boat to secure the moorings. Charlie slapped his hand in admonishment.

"Forgot to mention one thing, Mike, Jane comes with the boat" he said rather apologetically.

After four beers, and in this idyllic setting, Mike could only say one thing.

"Fair enough."

Jane, having secured the vessel, made her way down the wooden boards and waved to both men. "Hi Dad, who's this then?" she asked, extending her hand to Mike's outstretched arm.

Mike spoke first, and realised with his alcohol induced grin, fuelled by the euphoria of his recent purchase, he hardly looked the part.

"The new owner" he slurred slightly.

Jane looked at her Dad. Charlie looked at Mike. Mike looked at Jane, and all three burst out laughing. There had been no time for any ice to form, no time for Mike to consider if he really wanted to be working with a woman, the deal was done, so all three decided the best thing to do was to retire to the Nautilus Bar, to discuss the way forward..

The Nautilus Bar has a veranda that fronts onto the creek. As the sun sets, the locals arrive, all dressed in their Sunday best to watch the daily event. Mike just watched in amazement as the sun disappeared; the locals politely applauded, then they also went home. Mike had lived his life on instinct and coincidence, and he knew at that moment this was right for him.

The months had passed faster than any other time in Mike's life- not only had the chance meeting with Charlie Allington been his salvation, but, and Mike was still pinching himself, he and Jane had become lovers and in the last few weeks bought a small condominium together, overlooking the Four Mile Beach. Charlie was overjoyed; he had also lived his life by chance and was eagerly, if somewhat prematurely, awaiting his first grandson...

Mike Tobin had indeed found Paradise.

Chapter 26

Cairns Airport, Several Months Later

The Singapore Airlines 757 from London touched down right on time. Crammed with holiday makers desperately peering through the portholes to catch their first glimpse of the Antipodes, no one really noticed the two passengers leaving the first class cabin. That in itself was amazing for Dave Penny and Richard Sykes, known in the badlands of South London as the enforcers, had arrived in tropical Queensland in their best Saville Row threads, looking every inch city businessmen- not for them panama hats and floral shirts. They felt no need to blend into the environment, neither did they give a monkeys, for their sheer physical presence and intimidating looks encouraged the inquisitive to soon look away and avoid eye contact.

They sailed through Customs, although when asked the purpose of their visit, and replying 'vacation' caused a few raised eyebrows. A taxi was summoned, which took them to the Holiday Inn on the outskirts of town, where they checked in for a couple of nights.

Down in the bar on the first night, they were running through their plans again.

"So, tomorrow morning" said Penny, "We hire a car, we know this Mike fellow is just up the road, so it will be a piece of piss finding him, we spend a couple of days watching him, we have to assume he won't come back voluntary, so we've got to suss out how we persuade him otherwise."

"That's not going to be easy" Sykes said, " This isn't our usual target, we can't break a couple of bones or cut off an ear, but we need to get him on that plane

167

in one piece and willing to play ball."

"Agreed" replied Penny. "So, once we've got his profile we try every thing possible to persuade him that one million pounds is his for the taking, and do we know if he needs the money?"

"We know very little, well absolutely fuck all, apart from he's got some kind of boat, he takes the tourists out on, that's it" commented Sykes.

"OK," Penny continued, "There's one option, if he doesn't need the money now, maybe if his boat accidently caught fire, that might put a different complexion on his views."

"Not forgetting his house as well" Sykes added maliciously.

"That's a plan then, of course once we've had a good look at him and his lifestyle there's bound to be other avenues where he's vulnerable, let's just hope he's a normal bloke who would sell his Granny for a million, let alone do what he's best at."

And with that both men retired for the night.

The next morning the enforcers left the hotel and walked the short distance to the local Hertz Rental, where they picked up a decent Toyota and a comprehensive map of the area and then made their way up the Cook highway towards Port Douglas, still in their Saville Row suits and ties.

Forty minutes later, the Toyota pulled up in Wharf Street, Port Douglas. The two men walked into the marina, found a couple of local fishermen, who knew of Mike, and who pointed them in the right direction of Mike's berth. They soon spotted the Kiosk, and were surprised to see a young woman sunning herself in one of the tatty chairs that were parked along side.

"That's interesting" said Penny. "Who do you think she is?"

"Probably just the hired help, but if she's anything

more it could be interesting" commented Sykes.

They strolled past without making contact, not wishing to show their hand until they had surveyed the area. However, in their smart suits with the sun scorching the tarmac, they were drawing unwelcome attention to themselves. Jane had noticed them from the moment they appeared on the wharf, and thought it strange that they seemed so disinterested in their surroundings, but soon dismissed them as they disappeared into the car park.

The two enforcers had rightly concluded that Mike was out on his boat, so decided the best course of action was to wait and watch. About four pm Mikes boat appeared round the headland.

"This looks like him" said a very sweaty Dave Penny, "Shall we go and talk?"

"Let's just see what happens first" replied Richard Sykes.

Mike followed the same routine that he had learnt since acquiring the boat. Having waved farewell to the customers, he and Jane double checked the ropes which secured the boat to the dock, then headed off, hand in hand, passing within three meters of the thug's car, towards the Nautilus Bar.

"Well, now that's interesting," Sykes said, watching the pair as they turned the corner.

Penny replied, " They're obviously a couple, we didn't know about that, so that might change things, he's less likely to want to risk his freedom if he's committed to that woman, so we'd better get a plan together and assume he says no, but hope he says yes. However, there's nothing we can do in these strides, we don't want people remembering us, now it looks like we're going to have to get heavy," and with that Sykes reversed the Toyota and the two thugs returned to the Holiday Inn, Cairns.

That night in the bar, the two men sat hatching their plans.

"So we're agreed then" Penny was saying, "Tomorrow we go to the boat, we'll talk with the woman, double check she's his partner, then we book the boat for the next day. We go out to sea and tell the man what we need him to do. If he agrees, fine and dandy. If he says no and can't be talked round, we tell him no hard feelings, and we'll go elsewhere, then we'll get to him through the woman, that means we're going to have to snatch her,and hold her as ransom, the problem then is finding a secure place to secure her, we've got to reckon he'll be gone for several weeks so it'll have to be a good remote hideout, then one of us is going to have to stay here to mind her, whilst the other goes back with him."

"Fucking hell, that's a hell of a risk" replied Sykes.

"Listen, mate" came the reply, "We've taken fifty grand of Mouse's money, how can we go home and tell him it's a non starter and give him his dough back?"

"Jesus, this is going to get messy, how about if we have to take the girl, as soon as he's on the plane we kill her and dump the body somewhere out in the sticks, there's miles of bush out there where no one goes, then get the hell out of this country, that's less of a risk." stated Sykes.

"I agree, but this bloke Mike Tobin is no fool, if he agrees to come back he will sure as eggs is egg, want to talk to the girl regularly, also he's bound to have some heavy mates, it would be better for us if we give the girl back safe and well, less chance of him coming looking for us after its done" was Penny's answer.

"Yup, fair point, let's hope he needs the money, cos if he doesn't we're sure going to have to earn ours" was Sykes's reply.

The next morning the two men, now dressed in

more suitable attire, made their way back to Port Douglas, parked in exactly the same spot as before, and walked across to where Jane was sitting.

"Morning, love" said Penny cheerily, "Would the boss be around?"

Jane recognised the two men from the previous day, *odd* she thought *one day in suits then the next in shorts*. She decided not to mention this fact, but asked, "Who wants to know?"

"That would be telling, love" answered Sykes ,who had perched himself rudely on the other chair.

"Well you'd better tell me what you want, because he won't be back for several hours," Jane told them.

"We want to charter his boat, tomorrow if that's OK?"

"For how many?" Jane asked.

"Just the two of us" was the reply.

There was something deeply suspicious about this, Jane thought, yesterday these guys walked past in suits, then today they turn up looking like tourists. The only answer she could come up with was perhaps they were businessmen who were going to make an offer for the boat, but why the secrecy? She was also well aware that her new partner had a deep and dark past. Since she had known Mike, they had discussed their previous lives, but Mike had always said there was a lot of his life which he couldn't divulge, and she had respected that, but this was now giving Jane cause for concern. It was likely these two characters were from that part of his life he was trying to forget.

Jane went on the defence."Well, we're joint owners" she said (which wasn't quite true). "Tomorrow we're fully booked, in fact the next six weeks are nearly booked as well, I can squeeze the two of you in on most days, but it's impossible to let you have the boat without disappointing all the people that have booked already."

Dave Penny dug deep into his back pocket and produced a bundle of notes that looked like, and was, ten thousand dollars.

"Does this change things?" he asked.

Jane was not only offended, but by now getting worried. This happened in the movies, not in Port Douglas,

"That's not how we do business, you'll have to go elsewhere" she stated with as much coldness as she could muster.

Penny shoved the money back in his trousers. "We'll be back at four to see the boss" was his response, and both men walked off without any acknowledgement of Jane.

Jane was really worried by now, and found her hand trembling. Who were these two Brits who thought they could walk into their lives like this, make unreasonable demands and expect them to be met? She knew this was going to be big trouble, but didn't know what to do.

The hours that passed between the men leaving and Mike returning were the longest of her life, her imagination was running wild, and when eventually Mike turned the headland it was fair to say she had never been so pleased to see him.

Mike walked down the gangplank and realised something was wrong as soon as he saw Jane. She came running up to him, threw her arms around him, and in a sort of gibberish speech, told him the gist of what had happened.

Mike quietened Jane down and took stock of the situation. There were plenty of people across the world who would like to harm him, but also plenty who would want to employ him legally or otherwise. He was erring towards the latter when Penny and Sykes reappeared.

"You must be the boss then?" enquired Penny extending his hand.

Mike ignored the act of friendship. "Who wants to know" he asked.

Richard Sykes responded: "Mr Tobin, Mike, we've come a long way to talk with you about making you rich, and we have a little business proposition to put to you, but it's highly sensitive, so if we could hire the boat for a day, we could talk privately where no inquisitive ears are." He threw Jane a sneering look.

"Listen" said Mike, "There's no way I'm going out on the ocean just us three, I've never seen you before in my life, if you want to talk let's go inside the boat now."

Sykes and Penny glanced at each other; "OK" said Penny, "but just the three of us, she stays on the quay", nodding at Jane.

"She's my partner, she comes aboard with us, or you can fuck off," Mike said getting agitated.

So it was agreed, reluctantly, that the four of them should adjourn to the privacy of the boat to discuss the deal.

Mike and Jane listened intently as the two enforcers went through the story. They spoke of the Brinks Mat, and the events leading up to the incarceration of Mouse; they talked of Danny Gallagher and how he had also ended up with Mouse on Her Majesty's Pleasure. They told Mike that for one million pounds sterling, cash, Mouse was willing to pay for his early release, and he was willing to pay half of it up front, as soon as Mike had hatched an agreed plan. They spoke of the breakout, and the fact that how it would be achieved was down to Mike, but that any resources needed would be found. They recognised that he was the expert; they knew Mike had been specifically trained at the American school of SERE (Survival, Evasion, Resistance and Escape) and that he was the best in the business, they had researched well.

Jane had listened with growing incredulity, was this a weird dream, or nightmare? She felt her life was changing in front of her, but was transfixed. Mike was listening intently, weighing up the options. As alien as this was to Jane, Mike had been here before. Eventually Mike spoke, and it was not what Jane expected to hear.

"You started this conversation by saying there were three people to pull out, but all I've heard you mention is two, who's the third?"

Jane looked at Mike, he was talking like he was considering this madness, her world was collapsing.

"And how in God's name do you know so much about me, I'm restricted personnel under the Official Secrets Act, and will be till I die" continued Mike.

Penny delivered what he thought was the fait accompli.

"The third person is only a passenger, but he put us onto you, and Mouse has agreed he comes, it's an old colleague of yours Jock Wallace."

This time it was Mike turn to look stunned. Jesus this was almost blackmail, and that explained how they had the full insight into Mike's previous life. More to the point though, the unwritten laws of the SAS demanded you were always there for your mates, both on the battlefield and basically forever.

Jane looked at Mike, he returned the look, and she thought: he's *thinking about this, unbelievable, no way*.

"Mike" said Jane, "I need to talk to you alone, will you two leave the boat until we're ready?." Both enforcers nodded their agreement.

The boys had laid their demands out as well as they could, they were pretty sure he had taken the hook. Much to their relief his expression hadn't changed at all as they laid down the deal, he was indeed a very cool customer, and probably a formidable enemy. They left the boat and sat waiting in the chairs by the kiosk.

For several moments Jane and Mike sat staring out to the creek. Jane spoke first:

"Darling, whoever this Jock Wallace is, whatever he means to you, however much a million pounds would mean to us, please, please don't go."

She was wise enough not to threaten him by saying if he went they were finished, but she had already made her mind up, if he went they were.

Mike sat very still, for what seemed an eternity. He eventually replied: "Yes I'm tempted, but I never thought I would find what I've found here in Australia, I'm staying."

Jane crossed the cabin and threw her arms around Mike. "Thank you" was all she could say.

Mike spoke to the two protagonists back on board. "The answer's no," he said firmly "Matter's closed."

Both men shook their heads, they were sure they had sold the deal.

"Well there's nothing more to say" said Penny, and with that both men left the boat, returned to the Toyota and left the Marina.

Jane was relieved beyond belief, and hoped and prayed they could soon put this terrible encounter behind them.

Mike was not so sure.

Back in the Holiday Inn, the two Londoners were in deep conversation.

"Right then,"said Penny "We have no alternative other than to convince him otherwise, I'll get my brother Jason on the next flight over, you and him will have to stay here and mind the girl. I'll go back to England with Tobin and we'll get the job done the hard way" he told Sykes.

"Bollocks" said Sykes, "We'll have to hire a house or something out of town where we can stash her then, better start looking tomorrow"

The decision was made; Mike was going back, come what may.

Ten days later, Mike and Jane's life had returned to normal, the incident of recent days was all but forgotten.

Jane was in her customary chair next to the kiosk, the Marina was deserted and she never heard the Green Toyota pull alongside her. Before she realised something was happening, three men had got out of the motor; two of them grabbed her and manhandled her into the opened boot. The boot was slammed shut, and the car pulled off. The whole operation had taken less than fifteen seconds, and Jane was now effectively a hostage.

Mike returned at his usual time. As he rounded the headland his sixth sense kicked in, something was wrong, and as the berth came into view and no Jane in her customary position, he realised something was very, very wrong. He moored the boat, left the tourists to their own devices, and hurried down the dock where he confronted Dave Penny, sitting in Jane's chair.

"Hello Mike" said Penny "We meet again."

Mike stared at him, "Where's Jane" he demanded.

"She's going to stay with my friends while you and I go on a little trip." was the reply.

Mike's initial reaction was to grab the bloke's neck and snap it, which he was entirely capable of. However, his training kicked in and he backed off and considered his alternatives, then spoke in a very measured tone:

"Where is Jane, how do I know she's going to be OK? If I go with you I need guarantees she's safe and untouched, I will to speak with her every day, and if one hair on her head is harmed, I swear I will find you

want 176

and your accomplices, and I will dedicate the rest of my life to finding you, and when I do you will regret ever having set eyes on me, believe it."

Dave Penny looked into Mikes eyes, he believed him and he didn't scare easily.

"That's a promise, there's nothing to gain by hurting your girl, so here's what happens now- you put a notice on the shed saying due to family bereavement all trips are cancelled for the foreseeable future, you pick up an overnight bag from your home and we catch the nine pm flight tonight to Heathrow."

Mike reluctantly agreed, his mind was racing however; he had less than four hours to get Jane back before he was committed to leaving her alone in this country with two dangerous villains. He could easily overpower this ape, but he had no understanding of what arrangements they had put in place if he resisted; things looked bleak.

Dave Penny and Richard Sykes had done their homework well, they had ascertained that Mike and Jane lived alone, neither had children, so their sudden disappearance might cause some comments from any friends they might have, but if all went well Mike would be back before they were missed.

All plans have a flaw. Penny and Sykes's plan had one flaw and one piece of bad luck. They had assumed that Mike and Jane had no living relatives. That was the flaw, and the piece of bad luck occurred on their very first day in Port Douglas when they asked the fishermen if they knew of Mike Tobin. Jane did indeed have a live and very able bodied relative who happened to be fishing in the Marina on that day, when Penny and Sykes asked him of Mike's whereabouts. Her father Charlie Allington.

At eight pm that night a very heavy hearted Mike Tobin boarded the red eye to Singapore on route to

London Heathrow.

Chapter 27

Sammy Mc Ilroy's house, Hampshire

As Sykes and Penny boarded their Jumbo for Australia, John Illes's wife Cathy was passing through customs in Terminal One, Heathrow, on her way to make a rather shorter flight, albeit the mission was the same, to secure the freedom of the two villains currently incarcerated in one of Her Majesty's penal institutions. Cathy, under instructions from The Mouse, was on her way to Malaga to brief Danny's brother Sammy on the possibility of Mouse and Danny's liberation. Mouse, in his usual way, was thinking ahead and planning the outcome, he knew when the time came all hell would be let loose, and the harder he made it for the police to trace the events back, the better chances the trio would have of making it. At this point, there was no tie up with the SAS man and the potential escapees, although Jock Wallace was a concern, but that couldn't be helped, as long as there were no further coincidences, they should be long gone before any tie-ups were made.

Sammy had returned to England with Cathy almost immediately; he saw his role as a facilitator and minder, and brother or not he still owed Danny big time for keeping stum after the St Albans foul up. He knew whatever way the SAS man wanted to play it, he, Sammy, would be in a position to obtain almost anything the man would require, his contacts were still good and he had a lot of markers ready to call in. If the Army man was going to pull any stunts, he was the man to bring him into line.

Sammy's English country home, which Mouse had decided was the best location to plan the escape, was situated on the southern tip of the New Forest, the

179

nearest town being Brockenhurst, and a few miles from the costal town of Lymington from which the Isle of Wight was just a few miles and clearly visible. The house itself was discreetly located down a leafy lane with no immediate neighbours, in fact Sammy had never met any local residents, this being one of those areas where the property owners were either self made millionaires or blaggers, and neither parties were mixers, which suited Sammy just fine.

On this particular evening the house, was occupied by Sammy and Cathy Illes. They were awaiting the arrival of Dave Penny and his cargo from Heathrow. Sammy had considered strengthening his numbers, knowing the SAS man was likely to be a handful, but, and quite rightly reckoned he wouldn't be any trouble as long as his girlfriend was in safe custody down under.

Just after ten pm the front doorbell chimed, and Sammy answered it.

"Hello Dave" he said with some genuine affection, "Hope the flight was not too painful, and you must be Mike Tobin" he enquired, holding out his hand in a display of attempted friendship.

Mike just looked into his eyes and made no movement to accept the handshake, neither did his facial expression change, but Sammy sure got the message. Cathy came into the hall and quickly recognising the building tension: addressed Mike:

"Mr Tobin" she said in a level voice, "These circumstances are not what we wanted, however it's what we've got, the fact you are here demonstrates you are going to get my husband out of prison. Now you probably hate us all, and I don't blame you, we are holding your girlfriend against your will, and will continue to until my man and his two friends are freed. No harm will come to her as long as you do exactly what we require, but believe me, if I think you, at any time, are considering any type of double cross, or contacting the authorities or any of your ex army mates, I will have her fingers posted back here one at a time, so it's up to you. One other thing it might help the cause if we can at least be civil whilst we are all working together."

Sammy whistled under his breath, what a fucking tough bitch she could be when needed.

" You people are barking mad,"said Mike. "You really have no idea who you are messing with, and let me tell you this if one hair on my Jane's head is out of place when I get back, each and every one of you will regret this day beyond your wildest nightmares. Now, before we even start talking about getting these people out of the slammer, what I require from you is this. Whilst I'm here I want to speak with Jane whenever I say, and I want to speak alone. If at any time she's not there, for whatever reason, this job stops and you've got a problem."

Cathy, who had assumed control of this opening debate, considered this carefully. There was really nothing this guy could say to his girlfriend, now held in a remote shack in the bush, that could assist any type of escape, and in any case the boys down in Oz would keep an eye on that.

"Very well Mr Tobin, agreed" stated Cathy. "But when you call, all I ask is that my guys are in the same room as your girlfriend, just to ensure she doesn't give the address away or anything that might compromise this little agreement."

Mike nodded, and announced he would like to ring Jane right away. Cathy handed him the GPS phone and ushered the men out of the room.

"We're right outside, any funny stuff and the deals off," she told Mike with some bravado.

Mike dialled the number on the side of the phone and recognised Richard Sykes's voice on the far side of the world.

"Put Jane on" he told the thug, a few seconds later Jane spoke.

"Mike?" she asked into the phone. Mike swallowed hard and composed himself.

"Hi honey, how are you?" he asked anxiously.

"I'm fine, Mike, and you?"

"Listen honey," Mike said, "until I can get you out of there I've got to go along with these bastards, so here's what I want you to do, somehow I'm going to bust you out and when I do these turkeys at this end mustn't know, so when I do and you're free and I ring, I want you to mention your Dad, just that word in the conversation, and I'll know you are free, is that OK?"

"Sure." said Jane, "But be careful and don't take any risks."

Mike put the phone down, and for several seconds stared into space. Somehow he had to orchestrate two extractions, one from a Category A British Penal Institution and the other from a hideout some where in Australia, and as if that wasn't enough, the Australian breakout had to happen before the jail bust. The Gods of fate who had orchestrated this affair would have to play one last hand.

Mike switched the GPS phone off and called to the other two that he had finished.

Cathy entered the room. "We've kept our end of the bargain, Mike," she said, "so I suggest we turn in for the night and get down to business first thing in the morning. Your room is on the first floor, we're not going to lock you in, and you understand the stakes. All I would say is, no wandering about the house, the CCTV cameras will pick you up," and with that veiled threat Cathy wished the three men goodnight, and retired.

The next morning the four conspirators sat round the large pine table in the kitchen studying a large map of the Isle of Wight. Cathy was the first to speak.

"Well, Mike, you've had a night to sleep on it, any thoughts?"

Mike, having decided his hostile attitude would only ensure the other three kept him under intense scrutiny, replied with a civility that was a distinct change from the previous evening.

"Yes, but before I decide the best method, we have to agree some ground rules."

"Fair enough, go on," replied Dave Penny, who up to this point had remained remarkably quiet.

"Firstly" Mike stated "I figure the Island will have all sorts of cameras, vehicle recognition surveillance and the like, therefore we always travel on and off separately."

Cathy raised an eyebrow and threw an inquisitive glance at Penny and Sammy. Mike continued:

"When we get the boys out, and the shit hits the fan, every recording, every CCTV image on the Island, will be scanned and double checked, so we have to take every measure we can to ensure the police and prison authorities cannot tie up any associations. If at any time I'm seen with any of you three, and the police add it all up, I'm fucked for the rest of my life. This way, at least I've half a chance of getting out and resuming my life."

"That makes sense for you," said Cathy " but you can't seriously suggest we let you loose on your own, what's not to stop you phoning your old mates to go searching for your girl? Jesus, you could even go to the old bill and do a deal. Sorry, but that's not happening."

"What I'm proposing," Mike continued, " is you find a minder, but neither Sammy nor Penny, someone with no form or association with the police, someone

183

who is as clean as a whistle, but loyal to you, and not one of your small time petty thugs who draw attention to themselves either. I'd be happy with that."

Cathy thought for several moments. "I'm not over the moon, however I do know someone who can accompany you, but only whilst you suss out the Island. As soon as the fireworks start, they're gone." she stated.

"Wouldn't have it any other way" Mike replied.

Cathy took the phone and dialled a private number to a small terraced house in Dulwich. It was answered immediately. "Hi Mum" said Cathy, "How do you fancy a little holiday on The Isle of Wight?"

"If you think I'm going to visit that no good husband of yours, you're mistaken" came the curt reply.

"That's not it, Mum; I want you to look after a guest of ours for a few days, just drive round the Island with him, that's it."

"Ok then" Mum said with no more ado, "When do I come?"

"Dave Penny will pick you up in a couple of hours, see you at teatime." Cathy clicked the off button.

For the first time in a long while, Mike Tobin grinned. He had faced and conquered some of the most fearsome men that walked the planet, and now he was to be escorted, on his next mission by an octogenarian widow.

Chapter 28

The Isle of Wight

Cathy's mum had arrived the previous evening. It had been agreed that she be told Mike was looking at the possibility of assisting the Mouse, but not of his circumstances. Mike quickly realised she was the matriarch of the family, a wizened old bird who would not be messed with, but nevertheless an excellent cover for him to get up close to areas he would need to explore in great depth.

Mike had studied the access routes to the Island the previous day. There were several sea routes across, but Mike was aware if he was going to get the boys off by sea he needed the shortest routes possible, so he had selected two- one from Lymington, with a crossing time of thirty minutes, and one from Southsea at eighteen minutes. Mike chose the Southsea route, disembarking at Ryde, although the time saved on the crossing would be outweighed by the longer road trip, so he would return via Newport to Lymington.

It took Mike about forty minutes to get to the prison. After disembarking, he was driving the Ford Mondeo he had selected from the garage at the house; although he had been tempted by the Bentley it was too flash to be driving your Mum around. He hadn't spoken to "Mum" on the way down; this was not a time for small talk. Mike drove around the perimeter of the prison (or prisons, as the previous three prisons on the Island: Albany, Camp Hill and Parkhurst, had been amalgamated in the 1990s). It was as Mike expected, a daunting place with walls soaring skyward, forty foot or more.

Mike was in the zone, adrenalin surging through his

body as he analysed his options- knock out a wall with high explosive and have the guys ready to run for it? Unlikely to succeed, and even if he did get the boys, the alarm would be immediate and it would be impossible to get off the Island in time before a total shutdown was instigated. An airlift with a small helo dropping down into the exercise yard would be daring, but it had been tried before. Furthermore, since the 1995 escape, when three prisoners tried to steal a light aircraft from the local airfield, radar had been installed as part of the prison's upgraded security, so that any incoming air traffic could be detected at least five minutes before arrival, allowing the authorities to take action which meant getting all prisoners under lockdown.

Mike was already gyrating towards his preferred plan of action when, after his third tour of the prison's perimeter, he turned off the main A3020 which runs along and past the prison, into a small housing estate. The nearest houses to the prison perimeter were located in Sherwood Road, a street of neat semi-detached houses. Their back gardens were within sight of the prison walls, hardly an ideal spot to raise a family, but no doubt the prices reflected these restrictions. Mike drove down the road and noted two of the properties were up for sale. What luck, he thought to himself. A plan was hatching already.

Mike called the Real Estate Company and requested an immediate viewing of the one which was nearest the establishment; he explained he was only on the Island today and a cash buyer. Mike was actually very excited; he had temporarily and unforgivably forgotten about Jane, and his mind was racing with the opportunity he had found in this quiet little street. The estate agent arrived within the hour, having rushed round to the vendor's place of work to get the keys, explaining there was a cash buyer who seemed very keen. Mike introduced himself as a business man from Shropshire who wanted to move his dear old Mum out of London to a more tranquil location; after all London was not the place it was, what with all the immigrants that had swamped the place in recent years. The estate agent nodded sagely. Mike gave the place a quick once over, perfect, now the most important question:

"What are the neighbours like? It wouldn't do for Mum to have a disruptive family next door," he enquired. The estate agent beamed.

"Well Sir, you will be pleased to know, there's just a little old lady next door, about your mum's age, no disrespect meant, and she's totally deaf."

"I think we have a deal" Mike beamed. "I'll ring you inside twenty four hours to confirm."

Hands were heartily shaken, and the estate agent was on his way back to give the vendor the good news.

Mike was buzzing; he was going to build a tunnel, right from the living room of this semi, into the bowls of Parkhurst Prison, to a location within the confines yet to be determined, and take out three convicts right under the noses of the guards. He had built three tunnels before, all successful, and from where he was standing they had all been longer. The Polish were internationally recognised as the tunnel men and he knew several Poles who were ex Special Forces that could be recruited for this plan, and indeed had worked with Mike on other occasions. At this point Mike's thought turned to Jane and he came down to earth with the velocity of an asteroid. *This tunnels going to take six months*, he thought, *fuck it, how will Jane cope for that length of time*? Well somehow, he had to get her back before the tunnel was completed.

Mike decided he had as good a plan as possible, and decided no more could be done on the Island today. He was pulling out onto the main road and heading towards the Yarmouth ferry, when he spotted almost directly opposite the main prison gates, the entrance to St Mary's Hospital, he had a déjà-vu moment, Something deep inside him caused him to momentarily lose control of the car; he clipped a curb and steadied it, but the jolt the car gave was nothing to what seemed like the two thousand volts of electricity that were exploding in his brain. He had had a thought that was so outrageously insane it might work, and could be the answer to getting the three cons out in a matter of weeks not months. Whatever was going to happen, Mike was going to explore this second option and put it to Cathy who would surely want her man back as speedily as possible.

Chapter 30

Sammy McIllroy's House, the Same Day

Cathy, Sammy Gallagher and Dave Penny were seated around the kitchen table exactly where they had been when Mike had left them earlier that day. Penny offered Mike a cold beer, and Mike accepted. As he sat down barriers were coming down fast, Mike took a long gulp of beer.

"So, how was the Isle of Wight today? Were you able to come up with any thing concrete?" Cathy enquired hopefully.

Mike replied in a very measured tone, he had thought long and hard on the return journey about how he was going to sell them his plan without spooking them.

"I have had a very productive day, in fact it couldn't have gone better, and I have two options which we need to discuss. As extractions go, option one is the least risky but could take up to nine months to complete; option two is high risk with the possibility of getting them out in three weeks."

Cathy and the other two sat transfixed, this was more than they had dared hoped for. After just one day, this soldier was proposing not one, but two possibilities of getting the men out. It sure was looking like they had picked the right man.

"Go on, briefly explain both ways" Cathy almost whispered.

Mike talked through option one- he described how a tunnel would be constructed, how the spoil would be stashed in each bedroom, and how they would use akro bars throughout the house to support the additional weight on the ceilings. He spoke of recruiting a team of tunnellers from Poland, and why the Poles were the best at this type of work. He explained how the digging would take up to six months, but before that started how they would have to get building permission from the local council for an extension to the house, which would act as cover for the increased coming and goings during the tunnelling period. He spoke of the necessity of Mouse identifying a suitable point where the tunnel could breach the prison.

Cathy raised her hand. "Mike it seems like you've thought this through, and done this before, I'm impressed, now tell us about the quicker method."

Mike helped himself to another beer. This was his preferred way, but he couldn't tell them the whole truth for fear of the plan being dismissed out of hand. He started: "Option two involves a snatch." He waited for this to sink in. "Opposite the prison is a large hospital, my proposal is to get Mouse, Gallagher and the Jock into this facility and then get them out from there."

He was hoping this might suffice, but Dave Penny was quick to respond: "How the fuck do you propose to get three long termers into this hospital at the same time?" he enquired.

Mike knew this was the difficult bit. "In my line of business" he responded "There are times when we come into contact with the most unlikely of people. Several years ago, I made friends with a scientist who worked on contagious diseases; he worked out of the Ministry of Defence establishment at Porton Down. This was a highly secret Government establishment which explored unethical methods of warfare such as chemical and germ weapons. These people developed all kinds of lethal agents designed for mass killings that were to be used as an alternative to nuclear weapons. The government felt at the time, that such deadly silent weapons would be more of a deterrent than

190

conventional nukes."

Mike could see Cathy wasn't liking this, or where it was going, nevertheless he continued:

"The Porton Down project was shut down and my scientist friend transferred to the Hospital of Tropical Diseases in Tottenham Court Road, where he still works. With a little persuasion, my proposal is to obtain from him a virus which would be smuggled into the prison for the three guys to take simultaneously; it would have to be one with scary visual effects. The prison doctors would not risk keeping such people in the prison medical centre, and so would transfer them to a secure quarantine facility within St Marys Hospital. As they were being moved, we would take them then, and I would have a vaccine to administer, and away we go."

"Jesus Christ," was Cathy's response.

"So, and I may be being stupid here, but should any thing go wrong and you can't get them the vaccine, they die of some fucking tropical disease?" was Dave Penny's incredulous question. Mike knew this was coming. "And Jane dies with them, so I won't let that happen" was his calculated reply.

"And if all this comes off, there is still the small matter of getting off the Island, after all once you've grabbed the men, all hell will let loose, you won't make it to the ferry." Cathy remarked.

"That shouldn't be too much of a problem" Mike replied "There are lots of quiet coves along the coast, all within ten minutes from the hospital. I can get my hands on a small inflatable motor torpedo boat, which I can hide the boat in prior to the snatch, and we'll be across in no time. However, if we go with this option I intend to explore the possibility of arriving at the hospital in an ambulance and blag our way in under the pretence of transferring the guys straight up to London.

This would get us enough time to get across the water before the shit hit the fan, and maybe we wouldn't have to use force, but keep the boat at the cove as a fall back."

"Well, you've certainly got balls, I'll give you that." Cathy addressed Mike, "However, it's insane, and you guys might get away with such a scam in the Army but I'm not prepared to put my man at risk to this degree. Tomorrow I'm due to visit Mouse, so I'm going to tell him of both plans and that I'm instructing you to purchase the house, we go with the tunnel and that's final."

Mike was crestfallen, just when he thought he'd got through Cathy had put her foot down; his only hope was that Mouse would overrule her, but if he had read things correctly that was unlikely to happen, therefore he knew somehow he now had to concentrate on getting Jane away from her captives. He would have to wait until an opportunity arose where he could make a couple of calls.

Chapter 31

No 2 Visiting Booth HMP Parkhurst

As soon as Cathy entered the Visitor's centre, she had a feeling of deep unease. She hated this place, but never showed it to Mouse; it was after all her job to keep his dwindling spirits up, so when Mouse appeared she was all smiles. She sat in front of the glass window, and they both picked up the phone, the only way they could speak through the plate glass.

"Hello darling, how are you faring?" she asked.

Mouse forced a smile. Cathy could see something was troubling him deeply.

"I'm just fine," Mouse lied, "tell me about our friend, and make it good news please." he almost implored.

Although they were free to speak privately, Cathy went into a whisper, telling Mouse the good news that their captive was co-operating, and how he had a very plausible method to get them out. She also talked of the other option and laughed it off as total madness, just really to affirm to Mouse that even in his desperation to get out, she wasn't having anything so desperate and was prepared to wait the extra time for a safer but more realistic option.

Mouse looked long and hard at his wife, his eyes unusually rheumy and dull. Eventually he spoke:

"Cathy, I wasn't going to tell you, but now I have no choice. I've been having tests recently on what I thought was a persistent sore throat, anyhow yesterday the Governor called me up to his office." Cathy was beginning to feel her stomach knot up, Mouse continued:

"There's no easy way to say this, I've got cancer of

the throat and it could be terminal."

Cathy started to shake uncontrollably before dropping the phone in a flood of tears. How could this be, Mouse was such a strong man, he just wasn't the type to get a cold let alone the big C. Eventually Cathy composed herself enough to listen to what Mouse had to say, although right now she felt she was in the middle of a nightmare.

"Now listen Cathy, no one knows if this will kill me or when, but what I do know is I'm not going to get the help I need in this shithole and I'm not going to die in here. The Governor said he had spoken with the medics and I may have two years, maybe more, whatever the case, the sooner I get out of here the better my chances, so if I'm going to croak then lets make the most of what time I've got left." Cathy was devastated and couldn't speak. Mouse told her to leave and come back the following week when it had sunk in. She could only nod her agreement, and with that she unsteadily made her way out.

Cathy stood just outside the main prison entrance on the Clissold road. Still in a trance, but slowly regaining her thought process, she pulled out her mobile and dialled the GPS phone sitting on the kitchen table back at the house.

"Hello Cathy" Dave Penny answered.

"Put him on," Cathy ordered in a shaky voice. Mike took the phone.

"Its plan B, and it had better fucking work or you and your girl are both dead," Cathy barked and with that she broke down sobbing.

Chapter 32

A Pub Just off Tottenham Court Road

Mike Tobin had been shocked at how distressed Cathy had been when she returned home that night from the Prison two weeks ago. She had eventually opened up after a couple of very large brandies and told the men of the Mouse's condition. As tough as the men were, they were genuinely sympathetic to the plight Cathy was in. Mike tried reassuring her that the hospital job would be a piece of cake but it fell on deaf ears. Mike, of course, was very pleased with the outcome, although as a decent man he would not have wished it this way.

And so it was that Mike found himself sitting in The Dog and Gun, a plush pub a stones throw from the Hospital for Tropical Diseases, waiting to re-acquaint himself with Professor Don Gooch, who, despite his grandiose title, was still a young man in his mid thirties. Don had always loved working with the action men of the SAS, and secretly wished he had had the guts to enlist instead of following the academic route of Medicine. Mike remembered the continual questioning he and his mates would receive from Don when they were working at Porton Down, in fact the SAS troop, totally contrary to Army rules, as Don was classified as a civilian, once took him back to the barracks at Hereford and let him train in the infamous Killing House using live ammunition. It remained the highlight of Don's life, and Mike was hoping that episode would hold him in good stead for what he was about to ask.

Dave Penny sat in the corner of the pub. As much as Mike had tried to persuade Cathy to trust him alone, she had, wisely, refused and insisted Penny travel everywhere with him on the mainland. However, she had agreed that for the purpose of the operation Mike could speak alone with Gooch, as long as Penny was always in eye line.

Mike had worked out his angle of approach to the Professor, and was turning it over in his mind for the umpteenth time, when the man himself walked in. Mike, spotted him first and strode over to him, embracing him in a man hug as affectionate as if he were a long lost brother.

"Prof, you look great, you must have discovered a drug to keep you young" Mike quipped.

"You haven't seen the portrait in the attic," the Professor smartly replied, but this went right over Mikes head, Oscar Wilde was not his thing. Both men grabbed a pint and retired to the booth, where they could not be heard.

"Well Mike, as much as I'm privileged you've taken the time to look me up, I'm sure you've got an ulterior motive. Are you still in the unit?" Don asked.

Mike put his finger to his lips, more for effect than anything and lied, "Sure am, Prof, and yes, as good at it is to see you, we have a really tough challenge, ordered directly from the Home Office. In fact, and this is top secret, the Home Secretary is making noises about shutting the unit down, saying we're too archaic, and too expensive, so we've been given a mission to prove we can still operate in the most stretching circumstances."

"And you need my help?" Don asked, hoping the answer would be affirmative.

"Don, to a man the squad agreed that for what we've got in mind you are the only man we could and would trust. What's more, pull this off and the Boss says you can go up to Hereford and spend a week out on the Beacons in one of our hide and seek programmes." Mike was finding this lying a bit too easy.

The Professor stuck his chest out a few inches. Training with the SAS would be so cool, and give him street cred for a very long time.

"What can I do?" he asked.

This was the question Mike had been playing him into. Mike explained how the squad had been tasked with breaking out three members of their team who had been, placed, and now incarcerated, in one of Her Majesty's Prisons. The mission had been made harder by the fact the prison was Parkhurst on the Isle of Wight. Mike said that actually one of the squad who was in the stir the Prof might remember: Jock Wallace. Yes, the Prof remembered Jock from the Killing House; he had almost blown his head off in the dark, live ammo as well. Mike of course was banking on this.

"Mike," said Don "It sounds tremendous fun and so exciting, but just how can I help?" He was genuinely perplexed.

"Let me enlighten you dear boy," Mike said in his most endearing tone. "We need to get these lads into the hospital across the road, we need them all there together on the same day, so we need to fake an illness that looks so serious the Prison medics freak out, and ship them out for fear of infecting other inmates. So we need to infect our boys with some kind of virus that does that, then when we get them over the road, we give them a vaccine and whisk them back to Hereford, and the boss calls the Home Secretary with the good news there out, and that's where you come in, you up for it, so the question is, is there something available that you know of and can obtain that we can give them?" The sixty four thousand dollar question was out.

Professor Don Gooch, thought for a moment then looked sternly at Mike and uttered one word,

"Ebola"

Mike, for once rendered speechless, eventually found some words.

"Fair enough, you don't want to fuck about then."

Don looked at Mike, after several seconds both men broke into spontaneous and uncontrolled laughter.

The reason both men found the word Ebola so funny was not that it was humorous, far from it; to those in the know Ebola is probably the single most dangerous virus known to man since the Bubonic plague, and the eminent Professor was coolly suggesting they let it loose in one of Her Majesty's Penal Establishments. He truly was SAS material.

The Ebola virus was first discovered as recently as 1976, although it had undoubtedly been rampant on the African continent long before. It was named after a river in the Democratic Republic of Congo, where the first outbreak occurred. The World Health Organisation quickly categorised it as a Class A Pathogen, and soon after it became listed as a biological agent, capable of use in bioterrorism- no surprise as it is notoriously deadly with an up to ninety percent fatality rate. It was widely believed by the Intelligence services at Langley and Washington that the developments of these super killers were the main reason 9/11 was so successful for Al Qaeda. It was felt that the security services of the major world powers had all but abandoned the threat of an airborne or even nuclear strike, and such like, as these biological weapons were far easier to deliver and far more deadly, so they had taken their eye off the ball, just not expecting such an antiquated attack from the skies.

Don Gooch, however, was no fool, he understood Ebola well, and the symptoms were visually horrific. Red streaming eyes, a violent rash, high fever and external bleeding from the nose and ears- just what the SAS trooper in front of him required. Don also knew that whilst the virus was deadly, it was not airborne, and to catch it contact had to made either via blood, faeces, saliva or, as he was proposing, direct exposure. In other words, whilst he could instantly infect the three troopers, there would be little chance of this spreading to any other prisoner; it was controllable in his naive opinion.

The last piece of this bizarre jigsaw was that as far as the public at large were aware, there was no known vaccine, and that was why it had such a fearsome reputation. However, this was not true; a vaccine had been developed during the Porton Down years, but the Government had decided, in the interest of national security, to keep it under wraps, allowing several thousand Africans to suffer death rather than announcing it had a cure. The vaccine was a hundred percent safe, and the guinea pigs that it had been tested on had all returned to normal health relatively quickly, and that was why Professor Don Gooch was more than happy to assist his Army colleagues in this little scam; after all the disbandment of the SAS would ultimately be a bad move for the country. And, Don thought, if he could help in securing the future of the Special Forces Unit then ultimately he was helping the security of the Country. His conscience would be clear and in his own mind he was taking the moral high ground. Don Gooch had unrestricted access to both the virus and vaccine, within his workplace- perfect.

Don had explained all this to Mike, and Mike quickly realised that not only was the Professor up for this he was positively relishing the chance. Every officer in the British Army is taught that in warfare, whether open or clandestine, the theatre of battle can change; plans go astray, a sudden sandstorm, cloud cover, the introduction of nukes, a million unseen and unplanned occurrences, and this is when battles are won or lost. The commander who can change with the changes and turn them into opportunities will, almost always, be the victor, and Mike had recognised his chance.

"So, Don," he said, scratching his nose, "This seems almost too easy. We get one of the lads inside to identify a bent screw, there must be a few judging by the amount of drugs floating about in there, tell them we need some drugs smuggled in to our men, bung the screw a good drink, the boys take the goods, and hopefully go down with the virus all at about the same time?"

"Basically Mike that's it," Don replied, "However, to guarantee the lads start showing the symptoms pretty much on the same day, they would have to inject the dosages rather than swallow them. The incubation period is between two and twenty days which would be no good, so by intravenous injection as the virus would get straight into the blood stream they would all be a right state in forty eight hours. I'm sure your boys know how to administer drugs intravenously."

Mike was gradually building up to the big question.

"So Don, the lads get shipped out to St Mary's Hospital right opposite the Nick as soon as the prison medics realise they've got a big problem, once there we intend to grab them and make a run to the ferry. I don't suppose there's any chance somehow you could be around to identify the symptoms, and then call for an immediate transfer to your place, which would be me and a couple of the lads arriving in an ambulance. That would give us some breathing space and legitimise us getting straight on the ferry, and by the time people realised the scam we would be back in Hereford and the boss would have called in to the Home Office that the mission was a success."

Professor Don Gooch was capable of achieving

almost anything in the medical world, but spotting a scam in the real world was way beyond him, and his trust in Mike Tobin and the SAS was absolute.

"That can be arranged, I can always find a reason to visit our NHS hospitals," he answered, not for a nano second realising Mike Tobin had become a rogue elephant.

This was better than Mike could have dreamed of, and option two had suddenly become less risky than option one.

The rest of the evening was spent discussing the finer details- how long would it take Don to get hold of the virus? Don had unrestricted access to the secure room, would tomorrow be alright? The virus would be measured out in a dose relative to each of the three men's approximate body mass, to heighten the chances of the symptoms showing simultaneously. How long would the Professor need to set up a meeting or such like down at St Mary's? No problem, he would be known by reputation by the hospital authorities and welcomed without any prior notification. Wouldn't it seem suspicious after the break out that an eminent Professor from the Hospital of Tropical Medicine had arrived at St Mary's Hospital just as the first case of Ebola in Northern Europe was materialising? Yes, of course, but not in the first few hours; by which time the troopers would be back in Hereford and the Home Office would have alerted the hospital and prison services that it was all a covert operation ordered by the Home Secretary, no less.

The virus would be delivered to Mike in three syringes marked in separate colours to denote who got which one. Mike, having never met either Mouse or Danny, had to guess their weight on the spot - even the Professor might have got suspicious if he said he'd have to find out. As it happened, he figured two bank robbers were unlikely to come in at much under fourteen stone, even after a considerable time in the shovel. The virus would live comfortably within the phials for up to three weeks, this was achievable, and Mike knew Cathy was resourceful enough to get them inside well within this time. And that was that, quite unbelievably, in one evening Mike had a robust plan. Both men agreed to meet the next night for Mike to collect the goods. As they left the pub to go their separate ways Mike had one last thing to say, "Don, when this is done, I am personally going to ensure you become an honorary member of the unit."

"Who Dares Wins," quipped the Professor.

They parted into the night, each man very happy with the potential outcome.

Chapter 33

A wing, Parkhurst, 2 Weeks Later

As soon as Mike had returned to the house in Hampshire he told Cathy everything; he was in fact very pleased how quickly the plan had moved, and he was now anticipating being reunited with Jane in a few weeks. However, the events of the last couple of days meant he now felt confident enough to lay some ground rules of his own down. He told Cathy that as events were moving quicker than anyone could have expected, he felt at this stage, where there was no turning back, that half of the million pounds that had been the original bribe, should be paid into an account of his choosing, and this should be paid prior to the hospital transfer. The point was that if the bust out now went belly up, he would personally be banged up, probably for the rest of his life and there would be no point in harming or even keeping Jane hostage, therefore she should be able to rebuild her life with the help of the half million.

Cathy considered this, conferred with Sammy who was the bag man, and figured Mike's request was reasonable; after all it was obvious Mike had accepted that Jane would come to harm if he tried anything, and things had moved so fast that what could Mike do at this late stage? Cathy had therefore agreed that as soon as the phials were inside the prison she would have the half million transferred into Mike's bank. Although Sammy had wanted to pay in cash, Mike had said it was Jane's insurance money and it needed to be secure.

They discussed how quickly a bent screw had to be identified, and whilst Mouse was on board, how did the other two feel about injecting themselves with a deadly virus, with no guarantees they would get immunisation? Cathy had taken all these uncertainties onboard and arranged a fast track visit to Mouse the next day, agreed by the Governor due to Mouse's condition. Dave Penny was instructed to visit some old friends at an Essex scrap yard for them to obtain an ambulance and get it painted up, by which time Mouse would have nominated a Prison Officer who, for a nice little earner, would get the drugs inside. Sammy would sort him or her out.

The final handover of the guys once they were out was a little more tricky; no one had actually spoken of the aftermath and Penny was of the opinion that it was Mike's responsibility not only to get them out of prison, but out of the country as well. After some considerable argy bargy it was agreed that Sammy had the necessary contacts to facilitate a quicker departure from the UK than Mike, much to Mike's relief, and so the deal would be complete as soon as the men were delivered to the house, the quid pro quo being Jock Wallace was Mike's problem, and would stay with him..

Mike would take the Mondeo over to the Island the day before, and stash it some where discreet, so when he had the three men in the ambulance he could switch them over to the Ford on the Island rather than the mainland,the professor however was to be kept in the dark of this switch, so should he call the ferry company to warn them of the arrival of an ambulance arriving full of Category A convicts with a tropical disease, the ferry operators would not be looking for any thing else. Mike would do the crossing back solo as five large men squeezed into the Ford might draw unwanted attention. Mike now had both the virus and the antidote with him, so a date was set for two weeks time, if all went to plan.

John Illes looked drawn. He was due to start the first

round of chemotherapy in a few days, but his eyes had returned to life as he spoke with the other two potential escapees. It was association time on A wing and they had total privacy.

"This is it then boys, tonight's the night, we should have a celebration," said Mouse.

"Or a fucking wake" Danny replied, not quite grasping the irony in those words. When Mouse had gathered them together a couple of weeks ago and told them of the plot, Danny had laughed out loud, but soon sobered up when he saw Mouse wasn't joking.

"Not on your, or my life, am I going to jack up a barrel of poison, you can but I'm staying," was his initial reaction.

"What about you Jock?" Mouse enquired.

"To tell you the truth" Jock started, "I would be with Danny on this one, but, and it's a big but, I've known Mike Tobin for a long time. I've seen him pull stuff off that makes your little numbers look like corner shop shoplifting. I've watched him do things to people that would turn your stomachs. Failure is just not part of his vocabulary, therefore he is the only man in the world I would trust with this one, so I'm in, just one question, and I hope shitting yourself is part of the symptoms." All three laughed.

"Right then," Mouse had said, "Cathy's due back tomorrow, and she needs to know who's in and who's out, and the address of one of the bent screws. I'll tell her we want two doses, one for me and one for Jock, the screws will be easy enough."

"Three" came the reply from a very scared Danny Gallagher.

Mouse had secured the goods that day. The screw who had done the business had initially volunteered to help Mouse for nothing. Smuggling stuff in for the lags was a piece of cake and he and several others were making twice their pay easily; however, to have such a well respected villain as John Illes in his debt was far more useful than a buckshee monkey. Mouse, on the other hand, had insisted he take the drink from Sammy and that was that.

"Here's what we do," said Mouse, "when recreation finishes we go back to the wing, and we've got fifteen minutes before lockdown when we can meet in my cell. You, Jock, will be the doctor. I'm sure you know how to do this thing. For starters, I'm shit scared of needles and for seconds, we've only got one chance at this, if Danny or I balls it up there aint no second helpings, that's it."

"Yup, that's fine" replied Jock. It won't take a minute to do you both. What about the evidence, Mouse, if we're too sick to dump it?"

"Sorted" replied Mouse. "Jonny Reid, the screw who brought it in, will collect the empties in the morning. Cathy says the sickness will kick in twenty four to forty eight hours, so hopefully some time tomorrow night we'll all start to look pretty bad."

"Yes, lets hope the dose of Ebola I'm sticking in my veins does the trick and fucks me right up," Danny said with a deadpan face - more laughter, albeit exceptionally nervous laughter.

The bell sounded for the end of recreation. It was time to return to A wing for lockdown. The three of them assembled in Mouse's cell.

"No point in delaying things now." stated Jock, "Both of you, roll up your right shirts and tie your belts around your upper arms. Mouse, give me the syringes please."

Mouse reached into his trouser pocket, but his hand was shaking so much Jock had to pull them out.

"Fucking hell" said Mouse, "I wasn't this scared when we did the Brinks Mat."

Danny just sat ashen faced, his throat too dry to speak. Jock readied the first syringe, giving the deadly tube a small flick with his thumb to release any small air bubbles - this was going straight into the main vein, mainlining as the prison junkies called it, and Jock knew an air bubble passing through the heart could seize up the aorta and they'd be dead before the virus got to work. Without further ado, Jock stuck the needle into the now bulging vein of Mouse, withdrew the plunger slightly to ensure he was into the main line, and then pushed it right down, the yellow liquid disappearing into the body of Mouse. Danny was next and the same routine was followed. As Jock withdrew the needle from Danny's arm he said, "You know, on second thoughts..." SAS humour was not appreciated, so he followed suit and all three were now infected with the deadly pathogen.

Chapter 34

A Wing Parkhurst, the following 36 hours

The next afternoon Mouse received a visit from Cathy. As soon as she saw him she thought he looked distinctly flushed, but that might have been her imagination.

"Well did you go through with it?" she asked apprehensively.

Mouse nodded, he was undoubtedly starting to feel a little strange.

"Right then," Cathy started, "We've really no time to lose. As soon as I leave here, I've got to call Sammy. In forty eight hours, if what they've told us is right, you're going to be out of here and back at the house, you're going to be pretty sick but we can't afford to hang around. It will only be a matter of hours before the old bill realise what's happened, in which time you and Danny need to be in the air."

Cathy and Sammy had chartered a small plane to fly across the Channel. The owner was an acquaintance of Sammy's from the old days, and the hundred grand Sammy had bunged him was more than enough to ensure that the plane would be ready to fly at a moment's notice. Sammy had been busy, doing what he did well, fixings things, so the plane would land in Normandy where another acquaintance would pick them up and get them into Charles De Gaulle by road. They would have undetectable fake passports, supplied by yet another acquaintance, and then onto the final leg - Panama. Panama was the new Costa Del Crime, and Sammy had some colleagues there as well. A private hospital had already been booked for Mouse, it seemed all avenues were accounted for.

"What of the soldier boys?" asked Mouse.

"Not your problem," said Cathy ominously. "Sammy's sorting them out"

When Sammy had visited the Essex scrap yard, it wasn't only the ambulance he had asked the boys to sort.

With that, Cathy bade her farewell. It seemed almost surreal as she made her last passing comment: "See you at home in a day or two."

Cathy got out on the Glisson Road and rang Sammy.

"We go," was all she said as she entered her taxi back to the ferry.

Back at the house Sammy relayed the message. In truth, all was ready in anticipation. Don Gooch was already in situ at St Mary's, having arranged some impromptu lectures for the interns, the Mondeo was safely stashed on the Island, and the hooky ambulance was hidden in the garage, looking a dead ringer, with a souped up engine- the Essex lads had done well. It was now a question of Mike awaiting a call from the Professor.

The morning after Cathy's visit, the cells on A wing were opened as always, at eight am sharp. The form was, all convicts would muster on the wing's landing for a headcount before being escorted down for breakfast. This morning's rota was ironically led by Jonny Reid, as the warden in charge of counting the men, to ensure none of them had hopped off in the night. As he did the double take due to three cons being missing, a knot started to grow in his stomach; occasionally you might get one absentee due to sickness, but he just knew something was very, very bad this morning. The three cons missing were the three he had smuggled the drugs in for, and his immediate thoughts were that he had unwittingly brought in some stuff from those on the outside who wished them harm, and they had been poisoned. He didn't want to press the panic button just yet, he needed time to make sure his arse was covered if the worst came to the worst, so he called a couple of colleagues for a full cell search.

The first cell to be visited was Mouse's, and as Reid entered all he could manage to say was, "Fucking, fucking Hell." The sight that greeted him was some thing alien to anything he had ever come across in the past. Mouse lay on his back, his eyes red and bulging. He had obviously lost control of all bodily functions, blood was seeping from his nose, and there was a slight discharge from his ears - he looked awful.

Jonny Reid, gaining some composure immediately, called the Governor and the medical station and told them to get up to A wing as fast as they could. He entered Danny's cell - the same scene awaited him there. Reid couldn't hold his stomach back and emptied the contents right there on the cell floor. Wallace's cell was the same.

The resident doctor arrived first, took one look at Mouse, and almost gagged himself. This was well and truly out of his remit. The Governor was quick to react - a quick discussion between the doctor and the Governor followed, and both men concluded that whatever was affecting the three men was not good, not good at all.

"Governor, I'm going to call St Mary's," said the doctor, "whatever this is, these men should be in a quarantine unit immediately, just in case it's contagious. Best you lock down but evacuate this wing we can't be too careful."

The Governor nodded vigorously. The last thing he wanted was a full blown case of Legionnaires Disease, or whatever it was, on his watch.

Dr Reuben Goldstein was at his desk in the lower wing of St Mary's, chatting with Don Gooch about the forthcoming day's lectures, when the call came in from the prison, He listened intently.

"Tell me again, Doctor, very slowly and very thoroughly, the symptoms you are seeing. I have a colleague with me who is an expert in the field of unusual diseases, I'm putting you on speaker phone," he said very calmly.

The doctor described in great detail what he was witnessing.

"Stay on the line," instructed Reuben, "Don, I don't like the sound of this one little bit," he said to Don.

"Neither do I, Reuben, it sounds tropical, but that's impossible," Don replied, almost breathing a sigh of relief that the waiting was over. "Tell him we're on our way over and in the meantime they must clear the wing and no one else to come into contact with these people, and above all, no panic."

"Did you hear that, Doctor?" enquired Reuben.

"Affirmative" replied the medical man, "The Governor wants a word."

"Thank you, Doctors" the Governor said, "I'll make my way down to the main gate so I can escort you straight up to the wing."

Barely ten minutes later, Dr Reuben Goldstein and Professor Don Gooch were on A wing, Parkhurst, not believing what they were seeing. They had checked over Mouse, and were just finishing their examination of Danny. Don turned to Reuben, a look of disbelief on his face. "Reuben," he said, "It sounds impossible, and no doubt I'm wrong, but the last time I saw any thing remotely like this was in West Africa, where I attended an outbreak of Ebola." He was very convincing.

"Oh my dear God, it can't be" exclaimed Reuben.

"No, I agree, but whatever it is, it looks real bad,

and likely to be contagious. I'm not going to take any chances," stated Don, "I'm going to call London, and get an immediate evacuation of these people up to my place, where we have a specialised contamination unit. I can have our emergency vehicle down here in two hours."

Reuben and the Governor both agreed - the sooner this was someone else's problem, the better. Don pulled out his mobile, and dialled a number; the phone rang in a house in Hampshire.

"Doctor Gerry Hayes, at once," Gooch ordered

"One moment," replied Mike Tobin who held the phone for several seconds, and then replied, "Hayes speaking"

"Gerry," Don said solemnly "I'm on the Isle of Wight, Parkhust Prison actually, and I have a possible red alert." This was the code for a potential contagious outbreak of a foreign disease which could threaten the population, some thing the Hospital of Tropical Diseases were trained for but hoped would never happen.

"What do you need?" Mike asked, playing his role well.

"Get the emergency contamination vehicle down here immediately; get it to come straight to the main gate where the Governor will escort it to the sick bay, we have three potentials who need to be isolated."

"On its way," replied Mike, putting the phone down, and running out to the waiting vehicle as he gave the Cathy and Sammy the thumbs up.

"The specialised unit will be here in two hours," Don said to the Governor and his team, "Be ready at the gate to let them straight in, and let's get these patients off your hands."

All thankfully agreed. Don had made the call; it was more plausible to keep the three men on the wing rather than transfer them to St Mary's and then move them again, especially as it had been easy for him to get in, and he hoped Mike would understand.

Mike, kitted out in a rather bright high visibility uniform, was wondering why the plan had changed and he was now to go straight to the prison. Had the Prof lost his bottle? Was he walking into the lion's den about to be sacrificed - what the hell was the Prof playing at? Well, he wasn't going to run now; this was it, whatever the outcome.

Just under two hours later, Mike pulled up outside the main prison gates. They immediately opened, and a screw waved Mike through and pointed at a building in the far corner of the large open yard. Just as Mike pulled up to the sick bay, the GPS phone (which had never left his side) rang.

It was Jane making her regular call in; not the best of timing, but he sure needed to talk to her right now

"Hello, darling how are you?" he asked, and then his life changed again.

"I'm good, Mike," she replied, and then said, "Mike, as soon as this is all over I want us to go and find my Dad" - the coded message they had agreed if she was free. Mike froze, disconnected the call, and very slowly, very thoughtfully walked towards the sick bay.

Chapter 35

Somewhere in The Outback, Queensland, Australia

It was said that only the young men of the Aboriginal race of Australia went walkabout as a rite of passage, but this wasn't entirely true; it was not only the domain of the young, the older Aborigines often disappeared into the bush during the summer months, returning to the Northern towns of Queensland during the winter for warmth and ale. They could often be seen lying in the doorways of these towns, completely drunk; a source of considerable embarrassment to the townsfolk, whose opinion of these indigenous people hadn't changed much in the few hundred years since they, the newcomers, had arrived. And so it was the case with Dennis Tanami, a man of seventy years, and known as a shaman or medicine man to the Aborigines of the North. Every year he would wander the outback during the summer, eating the natural foods that could sustain a human life indefinitely. He would spend days on end in a hypnotic state, conversing with his God, and many sought him out for his mystic preaching and healing powers.

On this particular morning, he found himself sitting on a small ridge watching the derelict drover's hut where he had camped on many occasions previously. This time, however, there was something different about the ramshackle building. He had arrived the previous night, and as he approached he had felt that the building was different. At fifty meters there was a slight heat emanating from it, although there was no visible sign of life. His instinct told him there was something living in the building. The strange thing was if it was people why had they gone to so much trouble to hide themselves? No white people could get to this isolated spot without a vehicle, and yet there was no sign of life; so he watched and waited.

It wasn't long before his hunch proved right; the back door opened, and Richard Sykes appeared at the entrance. He looked around intently, was satisfied there was no one within the area, and lit a cigarette. Sykes would not have seen Dennis, even if he had known he was there, but Dennis saw him all right, and from the ridge could pick out his features with the clarity of the shaman.

Dennis knew by instinct that this white fella was a bad man, and wondered what he was doing so far from the town he obviously inhabited He wondered how many more of them were inside, and what they were doing. Dennis watched Sykes throw his butt to the ground and go back inside. He watched a bit longer, but nothing else moved. Well, whatever was happening, it wasn't his business and these type of men carried guns, so he collected his things, deciding it was none of his business, and wandered back into the bush thinking it was time to head for one of the coastal towns and find some grog.

Chapter 36

Macrossan Street, Port Douglas, Queensland

Charlie Allington was walking along the boardwalk that ran the length of Macrossan Street, deep in thought. It had been several weeks since his daughter and Mike had so suddenly vanished, and the mystery had deepened and darkened since the Private Investigator he had hired had reported back that Mike Tobin had boarded a London flight immediately after they both disappeared. Furthermore, the description of the person he was with fitted that of one of the men Charlie had met on the jetty looking for Mike. One thing was sure, Jane had not gone with him and there was no record or suggestion she had left the country, but that was the sum total of what the PI had found.

Jane was somewhere on the vast Australian continent, alive or dead. Charlie could only hope it was the former, but where to start looking? It would be just as hard if he followed Mike to the UK for answers, where to look for him? The local constabulary really weren't interested, as far as they were concerned it was a lover's tiff, simple as that, and if Charlie's daughter wanted to start afresh she could lose herself forever in Australia.

Charlie was oblivious to his surroundings when he walked right into another person coming in the opposite direction sending him flying into the road adjacent to the boardwalk. Dennis Tanami looked up from the tarmac rather pitifully; it wouldn't be the first time he had been assaulted by a white man. Charlie was beside himself, what an idiot; he could have sent this Aborigine into the path of a car. "Mate, mate, I'm so sorry," Charlie said as he bent down to help Dennis to his feet.

Dennis muttered some thing totally unintelligible and brushed himself down. Charlie helped him to his feet and felt even worse when he realised the man was an aborigine.

"Listen mate," said Charlie "How about a beer, it's the least I can do."

Dennis mumbled something, and sat down in one of the chairs outside a bar. Charlie took the gesture as a yes and disappeared inside, kind of hoping the black man might have gone when he returned, much to his shame. Charlie returned with the beers and Dennis nodded, which Charlie took as a sign of approval.

Holding the glass with two hands Dennis downed the pint in one go and looked at Charlie. *OK* thought Charlie, *he's going to milk this one and I'm paying, what the hell I just might join him.* So Charlie knocked his pint back, and took the glasses back for a refill. Dennis almost smiled. Charlie tried making small talk but all he got back was grunts, although he did get Dennis's name. Halfway through the third pint, Dennis looked at Charlie with his deep black eyes for several seconds, making Charlie feel decidedly uncomfortable, and then he spoke:

"Man, I can see in your soul you're a troubled man, there's a big black void where there should be light."

This didn't make Charlie feel any easier with Dennis, but what the hell; he was feeling over confident with the alcohol.

"Your right Dennis, so you want to hear my story?" he enquired of the shaman. Dennis nodded and looked at his now empty glass. Charlie did the honours, fetching the fourth beer, and then he began.

Once he started, it was like a great weight was lifting from him. He told Dennis the whole story, from

217

the chance meeting with Mike to the disappearance of his daughter. He was more lucid than the beer should have allowed and when he finished, he looked at the Aborigine not quite sure what, if any, reaction he would get.

"Fetch me a pencil and paper," the shaman said glancing at his empty glass. Charlie duly obliged on both counts and the shaman began to draw. It is said that when people see a ghost the hairs on the back of their neck stand on end, and as the shaman drew so did Charlie's. The alcoholic haze vanished as Charlie watched the face of Richard Sykes, the thug from London, materialise on the paper in front of him. When Charlie found his tongue and was able to talk, he stupidly but sincerely asked if this was what Dennis had seen in his soul. Dennis laughed.

"No man, not in your soul, in a derelict drover's hut outback."

Charlie was gathering his thoughts quickly now.

"Would you take me there?" asked Charlie, his throat as dry as the desert even after all the beer. "Sure man," said Dennis confidently, pushing his empty glass Charlie's way.

The next morning, Charlie was to be found in the boatyard, having taken Dennis home with him - not entirely for charitable reasons, he didn't want him out of his sight. He had spent the night rationalising the situation, and had concluded the coincidence was just too much; for whatever reason the thug from London had Jane captive out there in the bush, so drastic action was needed, and if he was wrong, well sod it.

He and two of his friends, Pete Fulcher and Den Lawrence had convened in Pete's shed. They had all been mates for a long time, and both Pete and Den were well aware of Charlie's plight. Charlie had rang both at five am and they were more than happy to meet and help.

"That should do it" Pete said.

"That'll bring a house down," Den laughed

"That's what it's going to do," Charlie said very seriously.

The two men had, since Charlie had filled them in, spent the preceding hours making and then welding onto Pete's already considerably robust land cruiser, the biggest kangaroo bar they could fit on the front. Dennis sat in the corner watching the goings on, whilst the two men threw him regular suspicious glances. He might be the saviour of Charlie's daughter, but he was still an Aborigine and not to be trusted.

At last they were ready to roll out of town, heading for the drover's hut. Charlie had estimated as best he could from Dennis that it was probably four hundred klicks North West. The last item to be loaded was a jerry can, full of high octane fuel which Pete used for his speedboat; Dennis looked on, slightly worried, suspecting it would not be full on the homeward journey.

Charlie had a plan of action- as far as he was concerned, Jane was a captive in the hut and if she wasn't it didn't matter one hoot what happened to the hood from London, he had it coming either way. Charlie had therefore decided to storm the building, hardly with the finesse of the SAS but nevertheless just as effectively. He had got Dennis to draw a layout of the building and ascertained there were two sleeping rooms, a living room, and a kitchen which led to the rear door where Dennis had spotted Sykes.

Charlie's plan was to drive the land cruiser right through the back door in the middle of the night. They didn't know how many people were in the building, but were confident they could overcome a small army, what with the shock the occupants would get. Pete and

Charlie had a baseball bat each, and Den was holding a Browning Hi-Power semi-automatic pistol. Pete made a mental note to ask him what the hell he was doing with it, after the forthcoming adventure.

The four men left Port Douglas, headed South to Cairns, then due West through the forty mile scrub until the road ran out, and then into the vast red desert they called the bush. Dennis navigated by a succession of hand movements and grunts, and no one else spoke. Eventually, after some five hours driving, Dennis signalled to pull over. Charlie looked quizzically at Dennis. "White man's hut over that ridge," said Dennis. He pointed to the small ridge he had camped on the night he saw Sykes.

"So why stop here?" Pete Fulcher asked gruffly, "We're probably two miles away."

"Wind in East, blow dust from car towards hut, they see us," the shaman said. Pete shut up.

The three men decided to park up and walk to the ridge. Dennis had done enough walking recently and curled up on the rear seat. There was just about enough cover on the walk to the ridge, in the unlikely event anyone came along.

"Unbelievable," hissed Charlie as they lay flat on the ridge looking at the ram shackle hut below.

"Not a sign of life," Den commented, "Do you reckon they're still in there?"

"They've got to be," Charlie said, with as much conviction as he could muster.

"Only one way to find out," was Pete's reply.

For a few more moments, the men lay there watching and hoping for a sign of life. There was none, which was disappointing. They worked out the angle of trajectory that Pete would drive the van into the back of the place. It was a bit chancy, as the building was so old they feared they might bring the whole structure down, burying Charlie's daughter in the process. However, this was a calculated risk as there had to be a large element of surprise to obtain the advantage over an unknown quarry. With that they returned to the land cruiser and waited for nightfall.

"Time to go" said Charlie. It was three am on an inky black night. Pete and Den had dozed lightly. Dennis had snored so loudly it was more likely to have warned the occupants of the cabin of their presence rather than any dust cloud, Charlie was bright eyed.

"Everyone ready" he asked. Just nods returned his question. "Right then, Dennis, wait here, back in a bit."

Dennis didn't need telling twice, this land, was his home, and whatever the outcome he could disappear as easily as he had materialised. Pete fired up the motor and cautiously drove the wagon around the ridge until they could just make out the silhouette of the hut. He pulled up and Charlie and Den quietly got out and made their way to either side of the building. They had agreed that if the roof came down on the cruiser there was a possibility they could all be trapped in the motor, and would be sitting ducks, so Charlie would take the left hand side and Den the right, a standard pincer movement in a game of paintball, and hopefully Pete would come in through the middle.

Charlie and Den were in position, and Pete gunned the throttle. By the time he hit the door there were two hundred horses screaming under the bonnet, the noise as he made contact was deafening- it sounded like a plane had hit the place. Wood and rubble flew every where, and Charlie realised they should have all worn goggles and face masks- this really was gung ho.

Charlie and Den were in the building simultaneously, and Pete was clear of the Toyota and right with them. The first person they came across was Dave Penny's brother Jason, who was on the sofa in the sitting room dozing. Whether he was an innocent traveller or a vicious kidnapper made no difference to Charlie Allington; he hit him with such force from the baseball bat that his left eye popped its socket and his nose split clean in two. Pete was already in the right hand side bedroom, and Richard Sykes, who had had a few seconds longer to realise what was happening ,was wiping the dust from his eyes whilst cocking the twelve bore he kept by his side in readiness for such an occasion, all to no avail. The baseball bat found the side of his head, breaking the jaw bone and leaving the right ear hanging by a thread. Den was into the second bedroom a second after that, pistol armed and ready; he saw a young woman hunched up in the corner and she looked terrified.

"You Jane?" he asked, like he was a seasoned professional. Jane nodded.

Den asked a remarkably sensible question next: "How many people are here?"

"Two men and me," said Jane almost in a whisper, and then, rather stupidly, Den said, "Wait here." He ran out, saw Charlie, and realised that both the men Jane had said were in the hut had been dealt with.

"Charlie, she's through there," he shouted and pointed. Charlie was into the room in an instant and saw the daughter he lived for curled up in the corner looking like she was twelve years old again and had just had the worst nightmare ever. She got up, crossed the floor, and flung her arms around Charlie, where she stayed for what seemed several minutes. Eventually, she released her vice-like grip and the tears flowed,

There was a hint of light in the East heralding the beginning of the best day of Charlie Allington's life, but it wasn't quite over yet. Charlie didn't want his daughter to see the mess they had made of the two kidnappers, and tried to usher her quickly through the remains of the living room. However, Jane was regaining her composure and stopped to look at Jason Penny, whose detached eye had been forced back into its socket, although it would never work again, and with great purpose spat in his face. Then she and her father walked out to the cruiser where Dennis, who had watched the events, was sitting in the rear seat.

"If it wasn't for this guy, we would never have found you," Charlie said, pointing at Dennis. Jane put her arms around Dennis and kissed him on the cheek.

"Thank you," was all she could say. Dennis almost looked embarrassed.

"Stay here with Dennis," Charlie told Jane, "I'll go back and talk with the others. We have to decide what we do with do those two bastards and we never spoke about how we would deal with them if we got you out, it all happened so quickly."

"Make it hard, Dad," was Jane's surprising reply. Charlie went to the rear of the motor and collected the can of fuel before making his way back to the shack; Dennis looked worried at this turn of events. Charlie walked into the remains of the building, and as both men saw the can of fuel he was carrying, they suddenly became very scared.

"Where's the motor you came in?" Charlie barked.

"In the far outbuilding," Sykes stammered.

Pete and Den wondered what was coming next. They hadn't bargained to be part of a murder- they thought Charlie was going to douse them both, before setting them on fire. However, Charlie marched out of the hut taking the can with him, and found the old Toyota the men had purchased back in Cairns. He poured most of the fuel inside, and the remainder over the roof and bonnet, struck a match and threw it into the car. The high octane fuel didn't need a second chance to do what it was made for, and several seconds later the car was a fireball. Charlie made his way back into the hut.

"Well, Den, Pete, what do you reckon we do with these two Poms?" he asked.

"Take them back with us and hand them over to the Federal Police" was Pete's suggestion.

"Leave them here to rot" was Den's.

Charlie thought for a moment, and then delivered his verdict.

"Right, we take them away from here, dump them in the bush and let them take their chances. If, and it's a great big if, they make it out of here, what can they say they've been doing out here, and if they die out here and they're found before their bodies are eaten, the authorities will assume there just a couple of idiot Poms got themselves lost and got what they deserved. How can they say any different?"

Den looked at Pete, both men nodded.

Pete said, "Agreed, Charlie; Den and me will take them into the bush right now. You, Dennis and Jane wait here, an hour's drive will be enough to confuse them, so they lose all bearings, then we kick them out and they're on their own."

Den and Pete roughly bundled the men into the cruiser and disappeared into the dawn. When they were out of sight, Jane spoke.

"Dad, have you got a cell phone?"

"Sure honey," replied Charlie "Why?"

"I need to call Mike," came the reply.

A few hours later Den and Pete returned having deposited their cargo in the middle of nowhere but kindly having left them a gallon of engine oil for when their thirst became unbearable.

Chapter 37

The exercise yard, Parkhurst Prison

Mike Tobin was in a state of shock. He had to think mighty fast- his girl was free, so there was no need to follow this through now. Jesus, he realised, he had already got half a million pounds, which they couldn't get back. But how could he get out of here without the others? The gates were shut behind him, and then there was Jock Wallace; he'd got himself into this mess but Mike couldn't abandon him, that was not Mike, and that was not the code of the SAS.

There were plenty of secret societies around that looked after their own- the Masons, the Church, the Law, but none came near the bond of the SAS. Leaving Jock was not an option. Mike had run out of thinking time; Don Gooch and the Governor were making their way towards him.

Don held out his hand. "Gerry" he said, "You've come yourself," looking at Mike.

Mike cottoned on quickly and composed himself.

"Well, Don, from what you said on the phone I figured it was the best move. If this thing is as bad as you say, at least I've had most of the vaccines which should protect me," Mike said convincingly.

"I can't allow you to take these three prisoners out of here without an escort," said the Governor. Don Gooch had anticipated this.

"Governor, look at them," he nodded his head towards the sick bay, "They are incapable of almost any movement, we can't expose any of your people to this possible virus, it's too late to inoculate your staff neither can we bring any attention to the ambulance. This is too sensitive."

He played his part well, and Mike realised the switch of venues was nothing more sinister than Don making the right decision that it was more effective picking up the three men from the prison confines.

"Point taken," the Governor said, somewhat relieved. "Let's get them into the ambulance then, there's no time to lose."

Jock, Mouse and Danny were wheeled out, all on separate gurneys, by three orderlies who were wearing breathing apparatus. Better late than never. They were quickly loaded into the ambulance. Don spoke to Mike:

"Right, Gerry, you make your way back to the ferry. I'll pick up my things from across the road and meet you down there."

The Governor interjected: "Would you mind just coming up to my office, Mr Gooch please? There are some forms to sign; this is irregular enough as it is."

"Of course," Don replied. "Gerry, get on your way" he said to Mike.

Mike pulled out of the prison and hit the road to the ferry. He had no more than fifteen minutes to think before he got back to the Mondeo; once there he had to transfer the sick men from the ambulance, then administer the vaccine which he held in a small aluminium case under the seat. He now had a choice. He could go through with the original plan to deliver Mouse and Danny to the house, collect his second payment, and split with Jock. He was well aware, however, that these bandits were highly unscrupulous and if they had decided to double-cross him at the last hurdle there would be little he could do, especially with Jock in tow. The second choice was that this could be payback time for all the pain they had caused Mike and Jane over the last few weeks. He made his decision.

The lay by where the Mondeo was parked came into view; thankfully no one was using it, and it was lower than the road, making it invisible to passing traffic. It was perfect to do the switch.

Mike pulled in and drew up next to the motor. He removed the aluminium case from under the seat, took out one the three syringes, and opened the rear doors. The three escapees looked worse than ever, and Mike thought it must be touch and go whether he was in time. Jock smiled weakly and managed to cock his thumb; well at least he recognised Mike.

Mike had no time to lose. Remembering his instructions from Don, he thrust the hypodermic needle through Jock's ribcage and directly into his heart. There was a small quantity of adrenalin mixed with the antidote- this would perk up the recipient and also get the heart beating faster, and thus the vaccine would start working quickly.

Mike helped Jock into the front seat of the car and quickly returned to the rear of the ambulance. Mouse and Danny wondered which one of them was next for the vaccine, but Mike did nothing. He looked at them both with a look of hatred burning in his eyes.

"I guess you two can hear me so listen up, you fuckers, you thought you could turn over the SAS. You're petty criminals that I've shit every day, you threatened my family and my life, and you thought you'd get away with it. Well I've got your lives right here in my hands, and all I've got to do is throw these two syringes on the floor and you're history, so any last wishes?" he spat out, as he lifted the syringes above his head.

Mouse and Danny were aware what Mike had said and were scared witless. They were going to die here, in the middle of nowhere, after all that planning and on the cusp of freedom. What kind of death would they have to face?

Mike loomed over Mouse, showed him the antidote

for the last time and then, right out of the blue, thrust the needle directly into his heart. He followed suit with Danny.

"The reason I'm letting you live is simple- I'm going back to my life, and I don't want a murder charge hanging over me. I've got half your money and you live, but, understand this, if I ever, ever hear that you or any of your henchmen are so much as thinking of coming looking for me, you and your respective families will wish you died of Ebola this day," and with that Mike walked out of the ambulance, locked the doors, threw the keys into the hedgerow, and got back into the Mondeo.

"Just you and me now, Jock" he said, this time Jock managed to cock both thumbs.

Speed was now of the essence. Mike had a plan- it was by no means foolproof, but he hadn't thought much of his final escape as he had been focusing on what would happen back at the house, fully expecting some foul play on his return. He had spent his time figuring out if there was trouble, how he would extract himself and Jock. However, that had been superseded by the events of the last two hours, so he gunned the motor to the ferry, calculating how much time he had before the balloon went up- providing he could get to his destination before this was all over the news channels, he might stand a chance.

The ferry was in, and Mike boarded with no trouble, so far so good. He picked up the M271 and then swung West onto the A36, heading up to Salisbury. In the town he stopped at the bank and withdrew as much cash as he could. Whatever happened, he was going to need a lot of money to execute his escape.

Heading north, he skirted Bath, onto the M4 westbound and then north onto the M5. Just over an hour later, and still nothing on the news stations (which struck him as rather odd), he pulled up at his destination. The Guard on duty at the Credenhill Barracks of the British Special Air Service did a double take.

"Mike Tobin?" he enquired looking startled "I heard you were Killed in Action."

"Well, I'm a ghost then," said Mike "Who's the boss these days?"

"The old man's still Major Morley," came the reply.

Thank Christ for that, Mike thought.

"Can you buzz him, tell him I'm here with Jock Wallace and we need to see him urgently?" Mike asked.

The trooper walked round to the passenger door, took one look at Jock, and whistled through his teeth, but said nothing; the SAS were trained to expect the unexpected. The soldier disappeared into the Guard room and came back a few moments later.

"OK Mike, he's in his office, go straight through the barracks, he's waiting for you." Another stroke of luck.

Mike pulled up outside the office of the Commander In Chief and told Jock to stay where he was. He grinned, as Jock was already perking up.

"Where the Hell do you think I'm going?" Jock managed to say, and Mike walked in to the boss's office.

"What the hell's going on Mike?" was the Major's greeting.

Mike tried to make light of it. "Good to see you too, Major."

"Sorry Mike, but I thought you were long gone, it's good to see you but something tells me you're not here to re enlist, in fact I can smell trouble," the Major commented perceptively.

"I'm not going to bullshit you, boss," Mike said, knowing that would be futile and probably ruin any

229

chance of the Major's help. "Jock and me are in a spot of trouble, best you don't know the facts, but the bottom line is we need to get out of the country just as fast as we can."

Mike hoped this would suffice and the Major was shrewd enough not to ask.

"Stone me, Mike," he said, "I daren't think what a spot of trouble is where you're concerned, but if you weren't in deep shit I know you wouldn't be here. Let me make a call."

The Major dialled the number for RAF Brize Norton and asked to be put through to the Station Commander.

"Hi Doug, Morley here," he said as the line connected.

"What can I do you Major?" came the reply.

"Doug, you've got a Hercules leaving today for Kabul, I understand you're picking up a couple of Scots Guards for burial over here. I've got a couple of passengers I need to get into Helmand pretty quick, has it left yet and if not can you squeeze them onboard?"

The Group Captain replied, "Must be your lucky day Major, we should have gone two hours ago but there's a sand storm over there, so we've delayed our flight for a couple of hours. The Met boys say we can go at three pm this afternoon."

RAF Brize Norton is used by the British Military and certain politicians of various countries to come and go into the British Isles by circumnavigating the immigration laws. There is, and always will be, a need for certain personnel to travel incognito and out of sight of the general public. and all the immigration checks designed to monitor their movements. And Brize Norton was that place.

"Thanks Doug, I'll have them there before it flies. I owe you one," came the reply. Major Morley looked at Mike.

"You're in luck, there's a C130 leaving Brize Norton in a couple of hours. I suppose you need your falsies," he said.

The term 'falsies' was used by the SAS in reference to counterfeit passports. Every SAS trooper had a number of false passports stored under lock and key at the Hereford camp. Never knowing what part of the world these men were expected to go at a moment's notice, they couldn't be held up waiting for the correct documentation to support their clandestine and highly dangerous occupation.

"Major," said Mike, "I don't know what to say, you've saved our arses."

"That may well be," the Major replied, "But I suspect the shit's going to hit the fan sooner rather than later, and I want you as far from Hereford as possible, by the way you weren't here today. Now let's get your falsies sorted and get you out of here."

The Major took the keys to the bunker where the passports were held and walked with Mike past the Mondeo. He looked in at Jock and then looked at Mike and just shook his head.

Ninety minutes later, the Mondeo with the two renegades pulled into Brize Norton and the C130 was on the runway and obviously waiting for them. A signalman waved the motor straight onto the runway and up to the rear doors.

"We've been expecting you guys," he said. "Climb aboard, we're ready to roll, give me the car keys and I'll park it up safely for your return, and good luck."

He saluted, knowing these were the guys who really put their lives at risk in hostile environments. Mike helped Jock out and they made their way up the ramp. He turned round to the airman and threw him the Mondeo keys.

"Keep it," he said as both men disappeared into the

carcass of the huge plane, homeward bound.

Chapter 38

New Scotland Yard, A Few Weeks Later

The Detective Chief Inspector was new to his role. His rise to the position he now held had been almost meteoric, especially as he had come up through the ranks the hard way. Partly he had been lucky, but also his tenacious approach to the job had held him in good stead. He was not one to give up and neither would he suck up to the brass; fortunately, when he had ignored orders from the top it had always paid off and here he was, Head of Serious Crimes, and reviewing a very strange case. The documents before him had been lent as a favour he was owed by a high flyer in Special Branch; the front cover was marked Top Secret Eyes Only and then The Parkhurst Break Out. It was this that had him intrigued.

He had been alerted to the breakout and the subsequent finding of two prisoners locked in an ambulance, within a few hours of the incident. He had subsequently travelled down to the Isle of Wight to start an investigation, and his first point of call was the prison Governor. The Governor had immediately agreed to see him, but had clammed up when the DCI had entered his office. He would not discuss the case and only referred the DCI to his superiors; no explanation was forthcoming and nothing could get the man in charge to open up. So the DCI had returned to London a very angry man. He had immediately demanded an audience with his boss, the Commissioner of Police. The Commissioner had made it abjectly clear that the case was closed, finished, and that the DCI was under threat of dismissal should he disobey these orders; and furthermore these instructions were directly from the Home Secretary, and there would be no chance of covering the DCI's tracks this time if he pulled his usual trick of ignoring a direct order.

The DCI had made some inquiries, having ignored his previous instructions, and eventually tracked down the documents that now sat on his desk before him. He opened the folder and read. The contents told of the plot to break out of the three prisons, and it went on to speak of the duping of the Bacteriologist Don Gooch by a rogue SAS man and named him. Furthermore, the plot was so heinous with the introduction of Ebola into one of Her Majesty's Prisons that the Home Secretary had personally ordered the case closed and had issued a D notice to all press agencies effectively banning any release of the facts to the general public. The Home Secretary could not afford the world at large to know Britain had an antidote for Ebola. Both Africa and the World Health Organisation would be up in arms, the Africans literally. Two of the three prisoners had been returned to prison, one was probably going to die of a different illness soon and the other would spend the rest of his days in Broadmoor, the penal institution for the criminally insane. As for the third prisoner, Jock Wallace, and the man behind the break out, Mike Tobin, they had fled the country; probably back to Australia where Tobin was last known to reside. By nature of what they had done their lips would be sealed. The Professor, who had been conned, had taken early retirement, having been forced to sign the Official Secrets Act; should he ever breathe a word he would be charged with Treason.

There was more, but the DCI had read enough. He wasn't going to let this one go whatever the Commissioner threatened. The DCI was an extremely resourceful man, so twenty four hours later he had gained enough information to take an early lunch break.

He walked the couple of hundred meters to the nearest Thomas Cook and booked himself the earliest flight to Cairns, Australia.

Chapter 39

A Bar, Port Douglas, Australia

Mike and Jock had had a relative easy journey back. After landing in Kabul they hitched a lift across the border into Pakistan, where they caught a scheduled flight from Islamabad to Hong Kong. From Hong Kong they flew 1st class, Mike having accessed some of his bounty, to Cairns where Charlie and Jane were waiting. The reunion was tearful and joyous. Jane screamed as Mike appeared through the immigration gate. He dropped his bags and ran to Jane's outstretched arms. Since that emotional return Mike had not let Jane out of his sight, but that was fine by both of them. Mike was troubled that no news of his adventures had reached the press, having no idea of the British Home Secretary's intervention.

Charlie had taken Dennis in and was starting to regret it. Dennis was beginning to make a nuisance of himself around town, but word had got round the small community of Dennis's involvement in Jane's return and he was tolerated, just.

It was a fine warm day, and the five of them had gone into town for a drink. Charlie, Jane, Jock and Dennis sat on the same table on the boardwalk where Dennis and Charlie had met those few traumatic weeks previously. Mike was inside at the bar ordering the drinks when a man ambled up alongside him.

"First beers on you Mike, if I remember right."

Mike turned to face the stranger, and the first thing he noticed was the little finger on the man's left hand was missing. He was looking into the eyes of Detective

Chief Inspector Toby Wakefield, formerly of The

Parachute Regiment.

THE END

Lightning Source UK Ltd.
Milton Keynes UK
UKOW040829211012

200891UK00001B/8/P